TWISTED FATE

By

PAMELA KENNEDY

Twisted Fate © 2016 by Pamela Kennedy

TMC Publishing

ISBN: 978-1-530757-78-7

ACKNOWLEDGMENTS

It is so hard to believe I am writing acknowledgments for my debut novel. I dreamt of this moment so much over the years, that it's hard to fathom that this is it. I am forever thankful to my God above, for already having a plan long before I even existed, and not taking my gift away when I didn't appear to be using it. Though life has a way of throwing curve balls and plans have a way of being changed, I know that it is only by Your goodness, grace, and mercy that I have fulfilled another one of my lifelong goals.

To Mommy and Daddy, thank you for instilling in me, BJ, and Nessi, that there is nothing we can't do. Thank you for giving in and letting me buy yet another book from the bookstore, even when I would read them in a day. I know I drove you crazy wanting to take my books everywhere we went from a quick car ride down the street, to the dinner table in a restaurant. I love you and pray that I have made you proud.

To my husband, my best friend, Desmond, thank you so very much for pushing me when I didn't push myself, and always believing that it could be done. I have always been able to count on you to give me the harsh truths and set me straight when I didn't feel like I could do it. I think of the time in August 2015 that I spent the WHOLE weekend in my office, getting my first draft completed. You held things down for me like I knew you would.

To my boys, Elijah and Ethan, Mommy can finally get some cuddle time in. I thank you for trying your hardest to understand when I couldn't join you at the movies, or come play outside, or wasn't at home to tuck you in bed at night due to writing. If I can teach you anything from this process, I pray that you know what it means to persevere and never give up on your dreams. There is absolutely nothing that you can't do, and I thank you for the extra hugs and kisses just when I needed them to make it through.

To my godsister, my ultimate sista scribe, Shatoya, we've written together since our middle school years; creating our stories in those spiral notebooks with clips from magazines and Granny Saulters' *JCPenney* catalogs, of our characters clothes, furniture, and accessories. I am ever grateful to God for our sisterhood over the years and even our partnership as writers. Though we did not complete this journey together, I take solace in knowing that you are rejoicing and are beyond happy for me, like this book was your baby too. I love you, baby sister!

To my sister-friend, Rae, I know you said you

remember hearing about me loving books more than toys, but without you and the connect for that book club meeting so many years ago, I would not have made the acquaintance of one the most awesome writers I know, who later became my mentor. Our special bond is evident that God always puts us at the right place and the right time.

To Jacquelin Thomas, my mentor…my sista-mama. Our bond formed over ten years ago, and no matter how "wordy" you say I am, there are not enough words for me to express what your mentorship and friendship has meant to me over the years. I know you always tell us you are "just being you," but the person you are is cherished by many. I thank you for instilling three major mottoes in my brain early: (1) put pen to paper, (2) writers write, and (3) give yourself permission to write it wrong. Thank you for the opportunity to let my voice be heard, through my writing, and being with me every step of the way to get the job done. I hope I have made you proud.

To my family (immediate and extended), friends, fellow disciples of Wake Chapel Church, fellow brother/sister scribes and members of New Visions Writer's Group, Sorors of the Alpha Kappa Alpha Sorority, Incorporated, and co-workers, thank you so much for the prayers, support, and understanding when I couldn't make a meeting, a rehearsal, or a night out on the town, due to meeting deadlines. I dare not call names because there are so many, I'm afraid I would leave someone out and each one of you, whether you know it or not, have had a part in the completion of my first full manuscript. Thank you from the bottom of my heart.

To everyone who aided in bringing my book to life. Fatou N'Dure for letting me muse with you for countless hours. Malachi Bailey, for the first real critique of my work. You tore it apart but I am grateful. Princess Gooden, for my book cover. You are absolutely the bomb! Michaella Neal for my author photos. Thanks, little sis. I'm praying for big things for you! For all those consulted on content for the book-Dr. John Jasper Wilkins, III, Charlene Lee, Toni Lee, and Barbara Garrison, I am forever grateful for your time and feedback.

And to my readers, I hope this is just the beginning of a great relationship between us and that through my writing you will be entertained, educated, and inspired.

Forever Putting Pen to Paper,

Pamela

TO MY KENNEDY BOYS--DESMOND, ELIJAH, AND ETHAN

I LOVE YOU.

CHAPTER I

"Michelle, I need an X-RAY for Brittany in Room 506; increased fluids for Demetrius in 510, and Ivory is due to come down from the PICU if all looks good on the last test." Nadya rolled off a litany of instructions to her nurse as she signed off on the last of her charts for the day.

"Yes, Dr. St. James," Michelle replied. "Oh, and what about Chase in 504? His mom keeps insisting that he needs more Tylenol."

Nadya glanced up from her file and rolled her eyes. At the point of supreme irritation brought on by hunger pains, she wasn't in the mood to entertain the rantings of an overbearing mother on an empty stomach. "Gently remind her that she has to give the medicine time to work. Keep checking his temp every hour."

Michelle nodded.

Nadya stuffed her laptop and stethoscope in her satchel. She should have been gone an hour ago to meet her cousin at Serendipity's to sample potential entrées for the reception. She was the Maid of Honor--the first time she had ever been asked to be in someone's wedding, so she had no idea what she was supposed to do, but Nadya was excited and willing to do whatever to make sure her cousin's wedding was perfect. She'd saved her appetite all day for this moment, to savor what was rumored to be the best cuisine in the area.

Nadya slipped on her coat, wrapped her scarf around her neck and grabbed her purse. She wasn't looking forward to the brisk January weather that clothed the city of Atlanta. She preferred warmer weather and looked forward to the summer season. Nadya walked through the doorway which led to the lobby of the hospital. She threw up a hand in salutation to Mr. Henry, the security guard.

He gave her an endearing smile. "Get some rest, Nadya. Gotta do it all again tomorrow."

"Uhh... don't remind me," she exclaimed over her shoulder as she exited the lobby and headed to the parking deck.

The cold pricked at Nadya's fingers as she buttoned up her coat while making her way along the breezeway.

Her cell phone blasted the all too familiar sound of Beethoven's *5th Symphony*.

Rolling her eyes, Nadya retrieved her cell from the Louis Vuitton satchel, and took a deep breath before answering via bluetooth.

"Hi, Mom."

"Nadya dear, can you stop by the bakery and pick up the French bread for dinner?"

"Mom, I told you I have to meet Chloe for taste testing this evening, and afterward I'm going home and soak in a hot bubble bath. It's been a long day."

"Absolutely not. Tuesdays are our family night and I won't hear of it. Plus I have someone I want you to meet. You remember Councilman Drake? Your father and I attended an appreciation dinner for him on Sunday, and met his family. His son Brian was so delightful and as soon as he told us he was in his second year at Bailey, Brown, and Barker Law Firm, I knew he would be suitable for you."

"Mom... not again. I can't handle another of your set-ups, and trust me, I'm fine being single." Socialite, Nadine St. James was forever the match-maker. Her lifelong dream was for her daughter to marry a man of status and wealth.

The phone LED flashed, signaling a second call.

She stole a peek at the phone noting Chloe's

name. *I must be in trouble because I'm late.* "Look Mom. I have to go. Chloe's on the other line."

"But sweetheart, I…"

"Love you, Mom. Call you later."

Nadya hit what she thought was the *Swap* key on her S5, and seconds later realized that she had hit *End* instead.

"Oh shoot…" she muttered. *I need to get to that restaurant before Chloe kills me…*

Umph…

Nadya's phone went flying out of her hand as her body collided with a hard physique.

Before she parted her lips to speak, he beat her to it.

"Pardon me," said the buff stranger in a suave masculine voice.

Her eyes rose to meet the brown, al-mond-shaped gaze belonging to him. Words es-caped her. When she found her voice, she uttered, "I-it was my f-fault… I wasn't paying attention."

He bent down, picked up the phone, and then handed it to her.

His hand brushed hers lightly during the ex-change, igniting sparks of attraction—something she hadn't allowed herself to feel in quite some time. The scent of his cologne wafted through her nostrils, mesmerizing her even more.

"Are you ok?"

"I'm fine."

"Glad to hear it. I need to get back to my daughter who's in the emergency room. Her mother is with her now."

A wave of disappointment flooded through her. The man was gorgeous and *married*.

"It's no problem. I hope your daughter's okay."

"Thanks. I'm sure it's nothing," he said. "Listen, I gotta get going, but if you have any issues with the phone, give me a call."

He then handed her a business card, which she placed in the pocket of her lab coat.

"You don't have to worry about it. I have insurance."

He smiled, showing a beautiful set of pearly whites before rushing inside.

Nadya's phone rang. She answered, saying, "Don't kill me. I'm on my way."

She picked up the pace and rushed to her car.

CHAPTER 2

Nadya whipped her Audi A5 into the first open parking space.

Before she could utter a word, she received an earful from Chloe, who was leaning against the trunk of her car with her arms crossed. "You better have a darn good reason why I've been sitting in this parking lot twenty minutes late for my appointment."

"Chlo, I'm sooo sorry," she apologized, using her nickname for her cousin. She turned to face her cousin, putting on her most pitiful pouty face, begging for forgiveness.

"Don't give me that..." Chloe waved her off. "Nadya, you know I might lack a lot of things, but punctuality is not one of them." She had her hands on her hips and her lips puckered out in a smirk, letting Nadya know she wasn't buying what she was selling.

"I would have been here way before now, but I had a few charts to sign off on, then Mom called with her usual matchmaking. Then on the way to the car, I bumped into…"

Chloe shook her head. "No, Aunt Naddi did not hold up our appointment trying to be Cupid. C'mon chile."

"I'm really sorry."

Her cousin burst into a short laugh. "Girl, it's cool. I'd already called them and told them we were running late." She spun around on her heels before taking off toward the restaurant entrance.

Relieved, Nadya smiled.

The sultry sounds of Jill Scott welcomed Nadya and Chloe when they entered the restaurant. The cylindrical architecture was ideal for all patrons, no matter where they were seated, to have an equal view of the dance floor at its center. It was surrounded by several cherry wood tables and chairs adorned with deep turquoise leather cushions. The outermost area was a level up from the main floor with booths lining the window clad walls, also with the same turquoise leather cushions. Serendipity did not open until three on Tuesday, so there was a steady flow of clientele already settled in for dinner.

Nadya's stomach growled in anticipation to the savory aromas coming from the kitchen off to the corner.

A hostess dressed in black with a turquoise and black bow-tie around her neck, greeted them.

"Hi, we have an appointment with Sabien for my wedding," Chloe said.

"Oh yes, Victoria is expecting you."

She stepped away briefly and soon returned with a young woman Nadya assumed was Victoria.

"Chloe, so nice to meet you," She greeted, then held an outstretched hand toward Nadya. "And you are?"

"Nadya St. James."

"Nice to meet you as well. Right this way, ladies." Victoria rounded the bar area and led Chloe and Nadya to a table near the dance floor. "Mr. Marshall was unable to make the appointment due to a family emergency, but everything is ready. We will bring out several options for you to sample."

On cue, two waiters approached the table with trays filled with tapas style portions of various meats and other mouthwatering offerings. Another waiter stood behind them with a tray of wines and cocktails in hand.

Victoria handed Chloe a navy blue folder with S.R.M. Catering embossed on the outside in gold lettering. "Inside," she explained, "are several different catering options as well as pricing, and a copy of the contract. Look things over, sample our assortment of goodies, and I'll be back over in a bit to answer any questions you may have."

"Thanks, Victoria," They answered in unison.

Before they said a word to each other, Nadya and Chloe tasted several different meats, starches, and entrées.

"Okay, I think this is definitely who you should use for the caterer," Nadya said. "I didn't like any of the food we sampled yesterday at Wynonna's Place. Whoever recommended this place to you must not have taste buds."

"The Secret Garden Restaurant was nice," Chloe stated. "I liked the salmon entrée, but the chicken was too dry for me."

"I've heard mixed reviews about the place. I think it's probably hit or miss with them."

Chloe agreed. "One of Justin's friends recommended this restaurant. This is who catered their reception."

"Everything I've tasted here so far is delicious."

"So who is Aunt Nadine's latest candidate for you this week?" Chloe finished off the bacon-wrapped shrimp and grits.

Nadya tasted the macaroni and cheese. "You know your auntie. She wants me to meet Councilman Drake's son."

"Oh, he's a hottie, but er um…I think he swings another way," Chloe said before taking a sip of her Cosmopolitan.

Nadya nearly choked on a piece of roasted chicken. She took a sip of her water.

"*Chloeeee.*"

"What? I'm just speaking the truth, and the truth shall set you free." Chloe laughed as she placed a heaping portion of sautéed spinach on her plate.

"You should be so glad that Aunt Audrey doesn't interfere in your relationships and lets you be your own person. I wish Mom would find a new hobby and just let me be. It's not like I have anything to offer a man…" Nadya's voice trailed off as she became lost in her thoughts.

"Nadya… don't go there. You don't know if that's the case. The doctor just said there is a lot of scar tissue." Even though Chloe was about four months younger than her, she always tried to be the *older sister* in their relationship.

"I'm just speaking things how they are…and I'm ok with that." Nadya retorted. "Don't get me wrong, I wouldn't mind having a handsome man to call my own, but it absolutely can't be someone my mother sets me up with. I won't even be able to get a kiss in, much less anything else with her interfering in things."

"That's Aunt Nadine for you. She means well though, Nadya, you gotta give her that."

"I know, but they never seem to work out," she replied. "I can do bad by myself." Chloe pulled a notepad from the folder Victoria gave to her, and jotted down the selections she wanted.

"Oh yeah... what's this about running into someone at the hospital?"

"I literally ran into this drop dead gorgeous guy after work." Nadya rehashed the details of their exchange to Chloe, and even more details of his physique and wonderful cologne.

"You better be sure to keep that card handy. I hate to hear about his daughter, but if that phone stops workin' we're gonna need a new one. How else are all the eligible bachelors gonna call you?"

"I can't stand you," Nadya shook her head in disbelief while grabbing her Mac lip gloss from her purse and gliding the wand across her lips.

After they have finished an assortment of desserts, Victoria returned to the table for follow-up questions, "Ladies, we hope the selection was to your liking."

"Absolutely," they announced in unison. Chloe pointed out the options she'd selected and asked any questions she had, as Victoria made notes in the tablet she was carrying. They were soon ready to head out.

"Mr. Marshall did call just before you guys finished up and apologized again for his absence, but wanted me to assure you that he will be in touch," Victoria announced as they made their way to the front door.

"Tell him thank you, and we completely understand. Family first," Chloe empathized as she and Nadya exited the restaurant.

Heading to their cars, Chloe revealed something that stopped Nadya in her tracks, "Oh, I think I saw Curtis today when I was leaving the wedding venue. It sure looked like him coming out of the St. Regis Hotel, but I couldn't figure out why he would be here."

Nadya hoped that she was wrong. Besides, why would Curtis be in town? It wasn't like he ever lived in Atlanta. He only came to visit when they were dating. Right now, he was the last person she wanted to see.

CHAPTER 3

Nadya turned off the ignition after pulling into the garage of the townhouse she shared with Chloe, and lowered her head onto the steering wheel and breathed in a heavy sigh, closing her eyes.

She was glad her cousin would be spending the night at Justin's, because she really didn't feel like having a discussion about Curtis and the past. She had not heard from him since he'd had the audacity to show up at her graduation from medical school. But before that, they hadn't spoken since that dreadful day.

Though they were in class on the same campus, she had to get to a place where she could exist with him, but without him. If not, she wouldn't have survived. Thank goodness for Chloe, who continued to push her forward, when all she wanted to do was put a pillow over her head, and stay in bed for an eternity with her blinds closed.

Nadya took one last deep breath before she exited the car. Every muscle in her body ached, and she craved a hot shower and sleep.

Inside, she slipped off her mules, and placed them on the shoe rack across from the dryer and slid into her Isotoners. She didn't even stop to peruse the mail Chloe left on the kitchen table, as was her usual ritual.

Instead, Nadya flipped on the light switch to retrieve a wine glass, grabbed a bottle of Moscato out of the fridge, and then headed to her bedroom.

Cloaked in darkness except for the moonlight shining through the window, offering a well-lit path to her first floor master suite. She hit the light switch next to her California king, turning on the pendant lights hanging above her bathtub. She placed her glass next to it. She removed the cork and filled her glass halfway.

Nadya ran a warm bath, adding a capful of bath salts to the water, along with a few drops of lavender oil.

She undressed, leaving her clothes in a heap on her closet floor. Nadya grabbed a white plush towel and matching washcloth from the linen closet and headed back into the bathroom. Before she stepped into the tub, to be consumed by the bubbly haven, she turned on her iPod to allow the sultry sounds of India Arie to fill the room.

Nadya stepped one foot after another into the bath and slowly submerged herself in the mound of bubbles. Her leg was extended so that her foot touched the nozzle of the faucet and the steady stream of water soon *drip-dropped* as the last few remnants made their way into the pool of water. Nadya naturally manicured hand grasped the wine glass and took a sip.

Her eyes formed thin slits as she reminisced over the day's events. The scent of lavender filled her nostrils and she smiled as she thought about Chloe happily preparing for her big day. The fragrance took her back to a time she remembered oh too well. She recalled them playing in her life-sized doll house, and their plans to have a double wedding. Chloe always wanted to wear a short form fitting dress, while Nadya dreamt of wearing a Cinderella style gown and a crown. Though now she shielded herself so much from being emotionally connected to anyone, she was sure there was no chance of that day coming.

Nadya's Nike shoes squeaked as she paced across

the hardwood floor of her bedroom. She spun toward her bed with a sliver of hope that what she'd seen an hour ago was a figment of her imagination, but there was no use. She'd taken every test available at the drugstore, to be certain. But whether it was two lines, a plus sign, or the word itself, they all read the same...

POSITIVE.

How was she going to tell Curtis? They had been careful every time, except the time they had been up late studying and gotten carried away and he didn't have any protection, but they had stopped prior to any release... hadn't they? And how was she going to tell her parents?

Her mother was already picking out color pallets for their wedding in the event he proposed. Even her father approved of Curtis, but neither of her parents would be none too pleased to hear that their daughter had gone and gotten herself knocked up before graduating medical school. Her mother would take it the hardest because she was all about status and public opinion.

When she'd seen the positive result earlier that morning, before class, Nadya screamed for Chloe, who came running instantly. Chloe cried and laughed with her, assuring her that Curtis would be there for her, because they were so inseparable, and she would support whatever decision they made.

After two agonizing morning classes, Nadya was

in a panic with sweaty palms and irregular heart palpitations, as the reality of her situation sank in. She took several breaths.

She and Curtis had plans for dinner that evening. Nadya was going to cook and he was bringing the wine. She would find a way to bring it up over dinner.

Dinner preparations were completed practically at the same time the doorbell chimed to announce Curtis's arrival. Nadya glanced at the elegant place setting on the table, and frowned at the wine glass next to hers. Her refusal to drink a glass of wine would catch his attention and most likely prompt questions.

Nadya went to the door and was met by a beautiful bouquet of white and peach calla lilies, with a hint of lavender intertwined… they were her favorite. She slowly pushed the flowers to the side to bring his hazel gaze into view.

Nadya kissed Curtis as he stepped inside the doorway.

It was hard for her to focus on what he was saying during dinner. Her mind was consumed with how she was going to tell him about the baby.

"Hey, are you okay?" Curtis asked.

She pasted on a smile. "Yes, I'm good."

"You don't like the wine?"

"I'm not going to have any tonight."

After they finished eating, they lounged in the living room to watch a movie. Nadya was sitting on one end of the sofa and he on the other, one leg posted up behind her and the other flat on the floor. Her long legs extended the length of the couch to meet him, feet in his lap, and as the tight but not painful grip of his hands offered a nice foot massage, Nadya decided it was time to tell him her news. "I'm pregnant," she blurted.

His fingers paused immediately and the dark brown eyes she had grown to love, widened in shock. He placed both his feet firm on the floor, pushed her legs over in slow motion onto the seat of the couch. He clasped both his hands together, placed his mouth on top, and turned his head in her direction.

Though his words were her own sentiments several hours earlier, what came next surprised her, "How could this happen? We were careful."

Nadya told herself that this was just the shock of it all, and tried to understand where he was coming from, but was soon annoyed when he said, "You're on the pill… were you trying to trap me?"

She held back her anger. "Umm Curtis, we are both on the verge of becoming doctors, and we learned about the birds and the bees long ago, so you know exactly how this happened. Don't make it like I made the decision not to use protection alone. Nothing is a hundred percent except abstinence."

He rose up from the couch and started pacing.

Nadya didn't move because she knew it was a lot to take in, and she also knew how having a baby could and would change their lives. She'd already thought about it though, and would put her personal goals on hold so that Curtis could finish his degree and residency. They could get married like they discussed—just earlier than expected.

She waited for him to respond, but he didn't. Instead he put on his shoes and coat, then left with no further discussion or decisions made.

A single tear escaped Nadya's eye, rolling down her right cheek. She used the back of her hand to wipe it away, only to have it replaced by more tears.

No, no, no Nadya.

She had told herself she wasn't going to do this anymore.

She had more than her share of tears over the years, but had finally gotten to a place where she was able to live, and move past it, even though a piece of her was gone, never to return.

She stepped out of the lukewarm water and patted herself dry with a plush towel. Nadya padded barefoot across the tiled floor, turned off the light, and dressed in her pajamas. She finished her wine and placed the empty glass on her nightstand.

Nadya yawned as she rolled back the honeycomb and gray duvet and slid under the covers.

Corrine Bailey Rae's *Closer* rang out through the surround sound as she settled in for the night.

Although her body was relaxed from the buzz from the wine, her thoughts were turbulent. It had been a long time since she was in this mind space—a place she refused to be again.

Nadya sat up in bed, as if she'd gained a second wind and grabbed her cell phone. Her index finger quickly scrolled through her contact list until she found the name she was searching for. She hit send and waited for the phone to be picked up on the other end.

"Hey… I know it's late but I need to see you."

"You know where to find me," said the husky voice on the other end.

Nadya ended the call, threw the covers back on her bed, and headed to her closet in haste to get dressed.

CHAPTER 4

The next day, Nadya rubbed her hand over her face in an attempt to wash away the weariness and prepare for her rounds at Peachtree Children's Hospital. She sipped her Starbucks ® Cinnamon Dolce Latte, as the elevator *pinged* its arrival to her destination. Her heels made a tapping sound as she exited and rounded the corner.

She entered the nurses station. "Morning everyone."

The duty nurse handed Nadya a stack of charts. "Things were pretty slow last night."

"That's good to hear."

She made her rounds, venturing from room to room.

When she arrived at room 504, Nadya was thrilled to be able to give Chase a clean bill of health because his mother worked her nerves. He was the last of her hospital patients, so she spoke with her nurse for a moment before leaving the hospital.

Ten minutes later, Nadya entered the building where her private practice was located.

"Morning," she greeted her staff before heading straight to her office. Her first appointment would be arriving shortly.

"This is a new patient," she whispered. Her nurse Candace left a post-it on the file noting that the little girl needed a follow-up appointment after a visit to the ER. No regular doctor but was referred to Nadya.

She turned on her computer monitor and checked for any medical information pertaining to her newest patient. Nadya frowned. The girl had been seen a number of times in the ER. *Why do people use the emergency room as a primary care provider?* she wondered.

She entered the last room, where she was met by the most beautiful brown gaze… a familiar one.

"Well, hello there beautiful. I am Dr. Nadya. What's your name?"

"Hi, I'm Serenity Reese Marshall," the little girl responded with a snaggle-toothed grin that could absolutely melt someone's heart.

"Nice to meet you, Serenity Reese Marshall,"

she said with a smile. Nadya turned her attention to the woman in the room. "Serenity's mom, I presume."

She reached out to shake the woman's hand, immediately recognizing how clammy her hand felt. Nadya instinctively rubbed her hand down the side of her lab coat, in an attempt to remove the dampness.

"Yes," she confirmed. "Vanessa Marshall."

"Nice to meet you. I see she was brought into the ER last night with a stomach ache, fever, and dehydration. Can you tell me how long this has been going on, Mrs. Marshall?"

"She complained of a stomach ache periodically over the last couple days, and I noticed she was losing her appetite and was somewhat sluggish. Then last night she had a fever of 101.5 degrees, so her father and I brought her in," Mrs. Marshall explained.

Her nervous pace did not escape Nadya's gaze. She could see the resemblance between mother and daughter. High cheekbones and mocha complexions mirrored each other. Though Vanessa's stature appeared all put together with her designer clothes and shoes, and flawless hair, something seemed out of sorts.

Vanessa continued pacing while wringing her hands together.

Nadya diverted her attention to Serenity, "So little lady, how are you feeling?"

"Okay... I'm hungry."

She smiled at the cute innocence of Serenity's response.

"I don't think it'll hurt if you have a happy meal."

Serenity shook her head from side to side, "Nooo I want shrimp, noodles, and white sauce."

Nadya arched her eyebrows in Vanessa's direction, "Expensive pallet for a four-year-old, eh?"

"She gets it honestly," Vanessa said with a tight smile. "Her daddy is a chef. Speaking of which... I have a meeting and will have to leave, but her father should be here at any moment."

A knock sounded on the door.

Nadya opened the door and struggled to maintain her composure. "Y-you must be Mr. Marshall."

Vanessa grabbed her purse. "I'm afraid I need to leave, sweetie. You're going to spend the rest of the day with Daddy."

"Okay."

Nadya was still trying to compose herself, from the shock of seeing the handsome stranger she ran into the day before. She could tell he recognized her as well.

Before he could utter a word, Vanessa left the room in a rush, leaving Nadya to wonder why she had nothing to say to her husband.

"How is your phone?"

"It's fine," Nadya responded. "This little angel is hungry, so I'm going to work quickly so that you can feed her." After a second review of the chart in her hands, she said, "It appears she had a bit of a stomach bug, but her appetite has returned and there's no fever. I would suggest watching her for the next 24 hours to see if she exhibits any symptoms."

His relief was evident. "Thank you, doctor..."

"St. James. Nadya St. James."

He smiled. "Thank you, Dr. St. James. I'm Sabien Marshall."

"Can I get something to eat now?" Serenity interjected.

Nadya smiled. "You sure can."

"Yaaaaayyy."

"Mr. Marshall, I was looking up your daughter's medical history. I didn't see where you have a primary care physician?"

"We are in between doctors. Her mother is very picky."

"I'd like to see her again in a month. Please stop by the appointment desk on your way out."

"Serenity, it was very nice to meet you. Enjoy your shrimp Alfredo."

She gave Nadya that big beautiful smile once

more, with a twinkle in those beautiful browns.

"Daddy, I like her. Is she gonna be my new doctor?"

"Thank you again, Dr. St. James."

She smiled. "I'll see you in a month."

Nadya left the room and went straight to her office. The tall and handsome man she'd run into yesterday was definitely married, but something seemed off between him and his wife. There was no communication or affection exchanged, which she found a bit unsettling.

Candace entered the office asking, "Did you notice anything weird about the mom? Vanessa Marshall?"

"She seemed like a worried mom," Nadya responded. "But there's something that doesn't seem quite right with her. I can't put my finger on it. It's just a feeling."

"I think she's bipolar," Candace stated.

"You think everyone is bipolar," she responded with a laugh. "Why don't you wait until you finish your degree in psychology before you start diagnosing people?"

"Girl, I'm telling you that woman has a problem."

"I'm not dealing with you today, Candace. I need to see my next patient."

Her telephone rang.

"Yes, Bernice," she said, referring to her office manager.

"Your eleven o'clock is a no-show."

"That's the second time. Make sure the parent is charged the fee. I need you to pull a chart for me. I'll come get it in a few minutes. The name is Chase Powell. I'm waiting on some test results that should arrive at some point today."

Her cell phone rang.

It was her mother.

Nadya ignored it. *I can't take you today, Mom.*

She checked her computer, then rose to her feet and left to see Bernice.

"Here's the chart you requested."

"Thanks," she said with a smile. "Since my patient's a no-show, I may run back to the hospital."

"Or you can grab a quick bite with me."

The sound of Curtis' voice sent her emotions reeling.

All eyes were on them as time stood still.

"Who is that piece of sexy chocolate?" Bernice inquired in a low voice.

Nadya struggled to find her voice.

"Is there someplace we can talk?" Curtis asked.

"In my office," she said.

The receptionist buzzed him in.

They walked in silence.

As soon as she shut the door to her office,

Nadya turned to face him. "What are *you* doing here?" She could hardly believe that the one man who'd turned her world upside down was standing here before her.

Curtis Matthews.

The man who had shattered her heart in tiny bleeding shards was in Atlanta.

CHAPTER 5

Curtis sat across from her, looking handsome in his expensive attire. Nadya gave herself a mental kick for entertaining the idea that they could have a civil conversation. She drank in his coal black suit, accentuated with a cobalt blue dress shirt, and necktie with a rippling diamond-shaped pattern of gray and varying tones of blue.

A sea of tension swirled around them.

Curtis broke the silence. "Thank you for agreeing to talk to me." He paused briefly and then continued, "You look even more beautiful than the last time I saw you."

Nadya smirked at him as she sat with her arms crossed over her chest. "*Whatever...*"

"The Nadya I knew was a sucker for a good

compliment."

I was a sucker alright, she thought to herself, but rather than share those sentiments she questioned him instead. "So why don't you answer my question, Curtis. *Why are you here?*"

He cleared his throat. "I'm in town for an interview. I wanted to let you know so you wouldn't be surprised when you see me around the city."

She tried to appear unfazed, "Oh… congratulations to you, but you don't owe me anything. And besides, the ATL is large enough that the chances of running into each other are slim."

"The position I'm interviewing for is at the surgery center with your father, so I'm fairly sure we'll be seeing a lot of each other."

The hand on the green stirrer in her cup, stopped the swirling motion, as Nadya processed Curtis's comments. *Why hadn't her dad mentioned that Curtis was a candidate for the open position?* She felt a little betrayed that her father hadn't said anything about her ex-boyfriend's potential move to Atlanta.

"Listen, I'm not here to make your life miserable. When your father mentioned you after our interview today, I really wanted to see you. I came to apologize."

Nadya felt like she was going to be sick. She was not ready to have this conversation with him…

not now… not ever. He'd had ample opportunity before but didn't bother to have so much as a word with her. She didn't expect him to take full ownership of the decision they made together, but she blamed him for walking out on her.

The hairs on the back of her neck stood up as varying emotions flooded her brain. "Maybe this wasn't such a good idea after all," Nadya said.

"I'm sorry for the way I acted back then."

"Curtis, it's a little too late."

"So you're not willing to hear anything I have to say?"

"I can't," she responded.

"As I said… I just came to apologize." Curtis rose to his feet. "It's good seeing you."

"I wish I could say the same."

He eyed her for a moment before leaving her office.

Nadya allowed herself some time to gather her thoughts and emotions before preparing for her next patient. Curtis was a part of her past and she wanted to keep him there.

CHAPTER 6

The sparse group of patrons scattered throughout Serendipity for Tuesday night dinner, afforded Sabien Marshall an opportunity to sit and review the metrics for the month. He also reviewed the details of the catering gigs booked, making notes here and there. Business had been really good and he was thankful, especially with all the drama surrounding his and Vanessa's divorce. He had fought it with everything he had, mainly because of his daughter. Serenity's birth gave his life meaning and he would do anything to ensure she was happy.

Things had been strained between him and Vanessa after their son, Jeremiah's death and for a while he thought their relationship was doomed.

They both dealt with their pain in their own way. Sabien threw himself into getting his restaurant off the ground, which meant less time at home, while Vanessa became a recluse.

He understood how she felt because it was the same for him, too. Eventually, Vanessa's sadness and longing for their son became less about her grieving and more of a pity party and wanting attention from those around her.

Sabien had one foot out the door until his Aunt Cori reminded him that marriage was not just something you threw away when times were tough. He and Vanessa went to counseling and were committed to getting their relationship back on track.

Over the course of the next year or so, things improved between them. With that came the news of Vanessa's second pregnancy. Serenity Reese was born on April 17th, 2009, and though he never thought he would ever have room for another child in his heart, the moment he laid eyes on his little princess with beautiful brown eyes—his previous reservations melted away and Sabien's heart burst with so much love and adoration for her. Even Vanessa was a different person. She began paying attention to her outward appearance again, trading her baggy clothes for more designer labels, and her bed scarf and ponytails for bouncing curls and highlights. She was very attentive to Serenity's needs and by the time their daughter was three—Vanessa had her involved in various types of activities from gymnastics to dance to cheerleading. Her energy level was through the roof. She gradually began traveling again for work which she did often before they were married. Life was good again.

However, it didn't last long.

She began experiencing major mood swings, wasn't sleeping and was increasingly obsessed with Serenity's health. Sabien assumed it was because they had lost their son, but couldn't get his wife to see a doctor. Their relationship deteriorated and he soon found himself in divorce court.

Jumping back to the present, Sabien reviewed Chloe St. James's portfolio. Skimming down the list, he noted she had a few questions regarding desserts and place settings. Sabien hated missing appointments, especially with new clients, but his daughter was at the hospital so he'd had no choice. He tried not to worry, but it was the fourth time she'd been taken to the ER over the past three months.

Serenity was not a sickly child at all; no complications at birth and no allergies. These recent episodes were becoming a pattern, and no matter how many times he told Vanessa that it was all in her mind—she never gave up until they ended up at the hospital. His ex-wife switched Serenity's pediatrician almost as often as she changed her shoes. She complained that they weren't diagnosing her correctly, and she knew it would only be a matter of time before something terrible happened to Serenity. Much of the time, his daughter displayed a fever or chills, but by the time she saw a doctor, the symptoms would be borderline normal or completely gone.

Sabien shook his head to himself, pushing the troubling thoughts to the back of his mind to get some work done.

He picked up his phone from the table and tapped in the phone number Chloe provided on her information sheet. Punching in the last digit, he hit send and waited for an answer on the other end.

"Hello, Chloe St. James' phone."

"Um. Yes, is Miss St. James available," he responded.

"No, she's not at the moment but can I take a message?"

"Yes, this is Sabien Marshall from Serendipity."

There was a brief pause, prompting him to ask, "You still there?"

"Yes, I'm here. You have no idea who you're talking to, do you?"

He looked at the phone in confusion. "Your

voice does sound familiar." Sabien glanced down at the name on the folder.

St. James.

"Is this Dr. St. James?" he asked.

She laughed. "Yes, how did you know?"

"St. James is not a common surname in this area."

"You're right. We're all related. Chloe is my cousin."

"Talk about a small world."

"Yes, it is."

A brief pause.

"How's my patient doing?"

"She's great."

"Well, I'll have Chloe call you back," she stated. "Your food is spectacular, by the way."

"So I take it you've been to the restaurant?"

"Yes, I accompanied Chloe to the taste testing. I'm her maid of honor."

"Oh, ok, cool. That's what's up."

"I'll be sure to give Chloe your message."

"Thanks. I appreciate it," Sabien said.

They said their goodbyes and he hung up.

Sabien sat back against the leather cushion of the booth, with his arms folded, phone still in hand. The few instances where he made Nadya's acquaintance, Sabien didn't have much of a chance to speak with her. But now that she was going to be Serenity's pediatrician, and was the maid of honor of his newest client, he welcomed the opportunity to get to know her better.

He went to rest his phone down on the table, but felt it vibrate in his hand. Flipping it over and glancing down, he saw her name. His patience for her had grown thin over the last six months since their divorce was final. At this point he only communicated with her because of Serenity.

He took a deep breath and answered, "Vanessa."

"Hi to you, too," Vanessa said. When no response was forthcoming, she continued, "Listen, I forgot to mention when we spoke yesterday, that Serenity has a follow-up appointment tomorrow with a new doctor. But I have a meeting that's been scheduled for months. I can take her but I won't be able to stay the entire time."

"I'll meet you there and Serenity can spend the day with me."

"Will do. Ta-taaa," she sang on the other end and hung up.

Sabien found it strange that Vanessa was always the one to discover issues with Serenity. Whenever she was with him or Aunt Cori, there never seemed to be any problems. As far as he was concerned, Vanessa was just being overprotective when it came to their daughter, especially after losing their son.

"Dia, I meant to ask, how did the dress fitting go with Aunt Naddi for the benefit ball?" Chloe inquired when she entered the kitchen. They spent the morning at the gym, then stopped to indulge in a mani/pedi before coming home.

"It went pretty well," Nadya responded. "But you know Mom and I can't be out alone together for a long period of time. She goes off rantin' and ravin' about how she wishes I would step things up in the fashion department."

Chloe walked over to the fridge, retrieved the chicken salad, and then grabbed a box of wheat thins from the pantry.

She took a seat at the kitchen table. "She does have a point Nadya. I try to tell you the same thing, but you know I give up after a while. You tell Aunt Nadine, anytime she wants to take me out and spend a small fortune on a new wardrobe for me, I'm game."

"By all means be my guest," Nadya replied. She had never been one for a lot of frilly, girlie clothes. But she appeased her mom on special occasions, and this benefit ball was her baby, so they found a nice strapless, sapphire dress—one that pleased both of them.

"I found a really nice one at Macy's and it was on sale," Chloe boasted.

"Leave it to you to find a good deal."

"Yeah girl. I'm all about a bargain," she said. "And you know I love to dress up. My bae and I are gonna be the talk of the ball."

Nadya chuckled.

"Hey did anyone call my phone while I was upstairs? I didn't realize I left it down here until I was in the shower already, and figured you would answer it if anyone did call," Chloe asked, changing the subject.

"Yeah, Ed McMahon called and said you were the winner of Publisher's Clearing House," Nadya answered with a laugh.

"Ok you got jokes, but I bet if I won, you would be right there with me, front and center holding up that big check at the front door." Chloe had always been one who liked to try her luck with the lottery, Publisher's Clearing House, slot machines, whatever.

Nadya always clowned her about jumping at her phone as soon as it rung, like she was about to win some sweepstakes. She suddenly remembered that Chloe had received a phone call, from the master chef himself.

"Sabien Marshall called."

"What did he say?" Chloe asked.

"He wanted to follow up with you and go over any questions you might have."

"Ok cool. I'll give him a call tomorrow. I don't want to do anything else tonight except get a little bit of pillow talk with my baby."

"That's what you want to do every night," Nadya teased. Chloe loved her some Justin, and he loved her just as much. They were a match made in heaven, she believed.

"Did I tell you he's the guy?"

"What guy?" Chloe asked.

"Duhhh...get your mind out of the gutter with Justin," Nadya said. "Sabien Marshall is the guy from the parking deck."

"Oh the guy who owes you a phone."

"Hush girl, there's nothing wrong with my phone," Nadya dismissed her.

"How'd you figure that out?"

"His daughter ended up at my office for a follow-up visit the other day. Her mom brought her, but he showed up before it was over."

"Oh so I guess we know he is married for sure then," Chloe assumed.

"Appears that way." She shrugged her shoulders and continued, "It's no biggie. I'm gonna go get a shower myself and call it a night."

Nadya wrapped her hand towel around her

neck, grabbed her protein shake and cell phone off the bar just as it vibrated, signaling an incoming text message.

She peeped down and quickly pressed a button to keep her cousin from seeing what it said.

"Un huh. I know that look… and you said that part of your life was over," Chloe said.

"What are you talking about?" Nadya's tone was nonchalant as she rounded the bar to head in the direction of her bedroom.

"You know exactly what I'm talking about. It's time for you to find someone to share your life with."

Nadya turned around, facing her cousin who was leaning against the bar with her arms folded, "Chlo, please don't start. We've talked about this time and time again. I'm not relationship material."

"But you can go and get your jump off when you need it, huh?"

Nadya looked down at the floor, not wanting to face Chloe's accusatory eyes. "I'm not having this conversation with you tonight."

"Look, everyone can't have the picture perfect relationship you and Justin have. But you're right. I can at least get some kind of pleasure from it and if Banks can give me that with no strings attached, then so be it. We have an arrangement."

She walked into her first floor bedroom, in need of a shower after their four-mile run, leaving Chloe in the kitchen. Nadya had no plans of meeting up with Wendell that evening, but she didn't feel the need to share that with her cousin. Outside of Chloe, she kept her intimate relationship with him hush-hush. For one, he was her mentor and friend.

When she graduated and moved back home to start her own practice, she had no thoughts of becoming involved with anyone. The day she passed her boards and was offered a job at the Peachtree Children's Hospital; she celebrated at a place called TJ's and ran into Wendell Banks. She was never one for one-night-stands, but she'd had plenty to drink that night.

Although he was ten years older, Wendell was handsome and muscular in all the right places--he worked out almost daily to keep his body toned. As they danced to a slow song, Nadya felt heat in places that had been dormant for quite some time. She gave in to his whims, and found herself waking up to breakfast in bed at his house the next morning.

They didn't see each other again until she arrived at the hospital for her first day of work and was introduced to him as the newest pediatrician on his team. Nadya worked hard to keep a professional distance at work.

Wendell was fantastic at his job, and she gained a lot of knowledge and insight as his mentee. However, he made it known that he wanted to spend more time with her, although he wasn't interested in marriage. His divorce had been an ugly one and he was still paying the price in hefty alimony checks. Nadya was fine with this arrangement because she also didn't want any strings attached.

She undressed and showered.

Afterward, she sat on her bed, thinking about the state of her personal life. At one time, she dreamed of marrying Curtis, having a nice house in the suburbs, while raising two or three beautiful children. He would be a top surgeon while she owned her own pediatric practice.

Wendell made it so easy to forget all that.

Nadya palmed her face to dab away the tears from her cheeks. Her phone vibrated once more, but rather than pick it up to read the text, she slid down further under the cover before closing her eyes and letting sleep overtake her.

CHAPTER 7

"So Miss Serenity, how are you feeling?" Nadya asked when she entered the exam room. She was surprised to see Sabien. She had assumed Vanessa would be bringing the child in.

"Fine," her tiny voice chimed in a sing-song kind of way.

"No more fever? Chills?"

Sabien shook his head.

"Awesome. That's very good to hear. Can you take a deep breath for me? I'm going to listen to your breathing with my stethoscope." Nadya placed the instrument on Serenity's chest and listened intently.

"And another," she instructed.

Serenity's chest rose up and down as she complied. "Now breathe normally, please." Hearing nothing that would cause any alarm, Nadya wrapped her stethoscope around her neck. She examined the little girl's ears and throat, along with her lymph nodes, all the while trying not to let her mind drift to the eyes she felt burning a hole in her back.

She gently patted Serenity on her leg as she reported, "You are in tip top condition. I guess that means you won't have to come back and see me."

"But why?" Serenity questioned, and her eyes immediately filled with tears.

"Oh sweetheart, I didn't mean anything bad. I was just saying you are all healed."

"But Mommy said you were gonna be my new doctor," Serenity whined. "I don't want to change doctors again, Daddy."

Sabien walked over to Serenity's side, to console his daughter, "Reese Cup, you are not gonna have to change doctors anytime soon."

Nadya's heart melted at the sight of this handsome man comforting his little girl.

"Serenity, you can still remain my patient, but as long as you are doing well, there is no need to come to the doctor," she assured her. "And this makes Dr. Nadya very happy, when her patients are doing well."

"Really?" Serenity asked and her eyes, previously clouded over with gloom, burst back to life with a bright glimmer.

Nadya smiled, "Of course."

"That sounds great," the little girl exclaimed, as she jumped into her father's outstretched arms, ready to leave.

"So now that I know your father works at a restaurant, I'm sure you had some great noodles, shrimp, and white sauce, huh?" Serenity nodded.

Sabien laughed. "It's her absolute favorite meal."

"Extensive pallet for a four-year-old, huh?"

"The life of a child with a chef for a father," he responded.

And a gorgeous chef at that, Nadya thought to herself. She couldn't hate on the little girl too much. Her parents, especially her mother, had introduced her to exquisite cuisine way before she could even spell the word properly.

"You should come to my daddy's restaurant. He can cook whatever you like. What's your favorite food, Dr. Nadya?"

"Hmm, let me see," Nadya tapped her chin in thought. "I love breakfast foods. I could eat French toast and eggs any time of day."

"Even at dinner time?" Serenity asked.

"Especially at dinner time." Nadya said with a laugh. "Maybe I will come one day and let your daddy cook me some of your favorite food."

"It tastes goooood," Serenity reached her arms to the ground to be put down. Sabien released his grip on her, and once to the floor, she walked over to the bench in the corner, taking a seat with her Doc McStuffins doll.

Sabien faced Nadya once again and said, "Thank you again for checking her out. Glad she has a clean bill of health. Vanessa will be relieved."

"I'll review her medical records from the other doctors when we receive them, and if there is anything that stands out, I'll let you guys know."

"Ok sounds good. Thank you," he replied. "Come on Reese Cup, we gotta get you to school." He grabbed her coat from the bench and Serenity got down and walked into it, with her doll in tow.

Nadya noticed how attentive Sabien was as he bundled his daughter tight in a purple bubble coat with a matching purple and teal toboggan. Her hat secured snugly atop her head, pressed her curly ponytails to her ears. He tapped the top of her nose in a playful gesture, and she grinned.

She can't help but think of the child she aborted, which brought on a flood of sadness and longing.

Sabien placed Serenity's hand snuggly into his. "Hey you should come to the restaurant sometime. Your meal will be on the house. This is the least I can do for sending your phone flying across the parking deck."

His smile sent butterflies soaring through the pit of her stomach like a schoolgirl with a crush. What was happening to her?

Nadya smiled. "I just might take you up on that. Be good, little lady."

Serenity nodded.

Sabien and his daughter headed to the left while she walked in the other direction to where her office was located.

She removed her pocket pharmacopoeia from her right outer lab coat pocket. As she did, a card the size of a business card came out, falling to the floor. She picked it up and read:

Sabien R. Marshall
Serendipity/SRM Catering
Owner

Nadya picked up the phone and dialed Chloe's number, "Girl you are not going to believe who was in my office today?"

"Who?"

"The owner of Serendipity. Sabien Marshall."

"He's the owner? I thought he was just the catering manager. How did you find out?"

"I just found his card."

"Are you serious?"

"Yes. Can't believe it's such a small world." Nadya remembered that Sabien had said the same thing the day he called for Chloe.

She talked a few minutes more with her cousin before they hung up.

A delicious image of Sabien formed in her mind. "If only he wasn't married," she whispered. Nadya didn't want to lust after a man she couldn't have, so she tried to banish all thoughts of him from her memory.

CHAPTER 8

Sabien snapped Serenity into her car seat, and got in on the driver's side. He put on the latest Kidz Bop CD and they rolled out.

He broke into a grin when he heard her singing.

As they entered the highway, his daughter blurted, "I like Dr. Nadya. I want to go see her tomorrow."

"Sweetie, you go to the doctor when you're not feeling well."

"I might feel bad tomorrow."

Sabien chuckled. "You look pretty healthy to me. Dr. Nadya says you're in good shape."

"I can only see her when I'm sick?"

"No," he responded. "I'm sure we're see her other times." Sabien thought about the exquisite specimen of a woman he had the fated chance of meeting up with again, Dr. Nadya St. James. He caught a glimpse of her curvaceous frame beneath her lab coat. She was blessed with both brains and body.

Twenty minutes later, Sabien pulled into the parking lot of Mahatma Academy. "All set, Reese Cup?"

He turned to find her knocked out, with head dangling over the side of her armrest, and the start of drool etched in the corner of her mouth.

He couldn't help but laugh. *That's my baby.*

He turned back to the front and pulled the key from the ignition.

Sabien got out and headed around to the back passenger door, to retrieve his daughter from her seat. He gently leaned her to an upright position, and removed the shoulder harnesses from around her. He adjusted her hat properly on top of her head, and pulled her hood on top as well, to keep the wind from blowing in her face. Sabien dabbed at the corner of her mouth with his thumb, wiping it on the back of his khaki pants, then picked her up and carried her inside the building.

By the time Sabien reached her classroom, Serenity was awake and peering beneath her hood.

"Good Morning, Serenity. We are so happy to have you back" her teacher, Mrs. Shar said.

"Morning," Serenity whispered.

Sabien gave the teacher a questionable look. What did she mean *back?*" Before he could ask, she was interrupted by another student.

"It's time to get your day started, sweetheart," Sabien said, sliding her down to the floor. She was still a bit sluggish from her nap, so he removed her coat.

"Alright Reese Cup. You have a good day and I will see you later on," he said, kissing her on her forehead as Mrs. Shar hung the coat in a nearby closet.

"Daddy, you promise to pick me up?" Serenity asked with an extremely worried look on her face. Tears welled up in her eyes.

Confused by her reaction, he bent down so that he was eye to eye with her. "Of course baby. I know you like to watch the clock, so I will be here around 4:30 or 4:45. Pinky promise."

Serenity curled her tiny finger around it, squeezing tightly.

"Now lose those tears, you know Daddy will always come back for you," he assured her, as she wiped her face with the sleeve of her shirt. He took a moment to gently kiss both of her cheeks and her forehead, and looked into her eyes, and it was as if he was staring in a mirror. He smiled at his baby girl, tapped her nose playfully which she scrunched up.

"Have a good day with Mrs. Shar and your friends. I will be back before you know it."

"Ok Daddy," she turned towards the interior of her class and headed over to a patchwork of carpet squares.

He gave a fleeting wave to Mrs. Shar and headed out the door.

Before he was able to make it out the front entrance, he was stopped by the administrator "Hi, Mr. Marshall, nice to see you. Do you have a minute for us to chat?"

Sabien glanced down at his watch, knowing he needed to be at the restaurant hours ago, but he always made time for anything related to Serenity.

"Sure, what's going on?" he asked.

Mrs. Darzi gestured toward her office for him to enter and take a seat.

"Mr. Marshall, I know that you and Mrs. Marshall are recently divorced, so I imagine it's hard when Serenity is sick so often. I want you to know that we will do what we can to help you both during the time."

"We just left the doctor's office and she's fine, so no need to worry."

"I'm glad to hear this. I know Serenity's been out several days over the past month and I was worried about her."

Sabien looked at Mrs. Darzi as if she had grown two heads, "What do you mean she's been out of school several days?"

"Mr. Marshall, I'm sorry. I thought you were aware that she had been out."

Sabien rubbed his hand over his face from his forehead to his chin, trying to calm himself down. As part of the divorce they shared joint custody of Serenity. "I had no idea, but Vanessa probably didn't want me to worry." He rose to his feet. "I've taken up enough of your time and I need to get back to the restaurant, but I'll be picking Serenity up this evening."

"It's good to hear because your daughter's been upset lately due to her mother picking her up late."

This explains why she wanted reassurance that I would be here, he thought. "If Vanessa's running late--just call me and I'll come pick her up. I'm closer to the school."

"Thank you, Mr. Marshall."

Reaching his car, Sabien got in and picked up his cell phone to call Vanessa.

There was no answer.

He hung up and dialed again, but it went straight to voicemail.

His phone vibrated in his lap, and he automatically assumed it was his ex-wife.

"You wanna explain why Serenity's missed so

many days out of school?"

"Sorry Sabien. It's Trish."

His face heated up in embarrassment, as he recognized the voice of his culinary school class-mate, "Ah Trish, sorry about that. I thought you were... I thought you were Vanessa. What's up?"

"Do you have anything lined up already for this Saturday?"

"Nah, not that I'm aware of; unless Chris has added something to my calendar since I was at the restaurant Saturday night," Sabien stated. "Why, what's up?"

"I have a major favor to ask of you. My mother has to have surgery on Friday, so I won't be able to keep this catering gig for Saturday." She contin-ued, "It's for a Benefit Ball sponsored by the Sur-gery Center. This is one of my big ticket clients. The lady in charge, is fierce, but she has an event planner who does the majority of the work--she walks around looking pretty and just signs the checks."

Though Sabien's preference was down home cuisine, he also had experience with upscale dish-es. He considered the opportunity. "Ok, I'll do it. But you better have everything lined up Trish, down to the swirl design on the petit fours."

She laughed, "Great. Of course you will design the swirls on your own petit fours. This is all you, man. I'll inform the event planner and have her contact you. In the meantime, I will send over the menu. You are a lifesaver, Sabien. I owe you."

"Yes, you do," he responded. "Again."

She laughed. "You're right. This is the second time you've had to bail me out. I'm in the process of hiring two new chefs, so this should help."

"I wish your mom a speedy recovery from her surgery."

When the call ended, Sabien made his way to the restaurant.

CHAPTER 9

No matter how crazy her mom drove her every February, Nadya had to give it to her. She sure knew how to throw a mean party. The Surgeon's Benefit Ball had been an annual affair for the last five years, as a means for local surgeons to be recognized for their contributions to the medical field. It started off as a smaller affair, but had grown in epic proportion, with people coming from miles around to get in on the festivities.

Each year it was more glamorous with elaborate themes. This year, she had turned the Founder's Hall into a movie star's dream. The sidewalk leading to the entrance was lined with a red carpet and white lights. The magnolia trees that aligned the sidewalk were adorned with lights as well. The steps that led into the entryway, were flanked on both sides by two massive Oscar-like statues, and a banner was draped off the overhang that read: A NIGHT AT THE OSCARS! 5TH ANNUAL SURGEON'S BALL. The red carpet extended up into the foyer of the exquisite hall, and led to a corridor of elevators.

Having arrived together in a limo commissioned by her mother, Nadya, Chloe, and Justin moved within the sea of people.

Nadya admired the gorgeous fashions worn by the attendees—she had to admit that the doctors and nurses cleaned up well.

She eyed her cousin and smiled, because she knew Chloe had been waiting for months for this day to come; almost as much as her wedding day.

The subtle ding of the elevator signaled they had arrived and the doors slid open.

They found themselves stepping out into the outer wing of the grand ballroom. Camera's flashing made them feel like movie stars.

After they finally escaped the makeshift paparazzi, the trio made their way into the interior of the room.

Nadya's eyes were immediately consumed with the regalia of the space. The ambiance of the Hall itself, with its crystal chandeliers and soaring cathedral ceilings, created just the right atmosphere with little to no additional embellishments. However, Nadine had added her own signature touch with an assortment of floating candle arrangements and multi-tiered centerpieces that boasted with dozens of stargazer lilies, intertwined with vines of ivy and whimsical piping.

After their seat assignments were confirmed, the trio maneuvered through the field of tails and flowing gowns to their table. They crossed over the tiled dance floor, and arrived at their table, just to the left of the podium. It was situated steps away from a dramatic staircase that opened up to two separate loft areas; one where the DJ was set-up for the party hour, and the other, where melodious chords were played by a pianist and accompanying musicians.

Chloe's parents, Uncle Nathan and Aunt Audrey, had already arrived and rose to greet them.

"Hello my beautiful ladies," Uncle Nathan circled the table to hug both Chloe and Nadya, and acknowledged Justin with a firm handshake. Aunt Audrey wasn't far behind.

"Hi Daddy," Chloe said.

"Hi Uncle Nate."

"You girls look beautiful. And you don't look so bad yourself Justin," Aunt Audrey commented with a kiss on the cheek to each of them.

"Aunt Naddi did the dang thang, didn't she?" Chloe commented with a snap as she took a seat in front of her place card with the assistance of Justin.

He in turn pulled Nadya's chair out, and offered her a seat. She grinned at him appreciatively, although deep down inside she wished she had her own plus one to do that for her. She hated being a third wheel.

"Yes she did. This place looks exquisite," Aunt Audrey replied.

"Have you guys seen my mom and dad," Nadya asked.

"Yes they were over here not too long ago, but have since been weaving in out of the crowd mingling with folk," Nathan confirmed.

Chloe settled into her seat and perused the remaining place cards.

"I don't know how Nadine does this every year. I would be out of commission for a month after this," Aunt Audrey commented. "The décor… the music… and let's not forget to mention the food. Chloe, looks like we're gonna get another opportunity to sample your wedding caterer's cuisine."

"Why do you say that?" Nadya chimed in before Chloe could speak.

"Oh, you didn't know? SRM catering is responsible for the food tonight," Aunt Audrey confirmed, as she poked at a strawberry on her tiny appetizer plate with a toothpick.

"Are you sure?" Nadya inquired. A wave of excitement washed over her at the thought of seeing Sabien again.

She quickly admonished herself--the man was married. *Get a grip, girl.*

Her aunt nodded. "Yes, as a matter of fact, there is one of the crew over there, with the SRM initials embellished on his coat."

Chloe and Nadya's heads turned simultaneously and there in the flesh, was Sabien Marshall.

OMG. Even in his Chef's garb, he was easy on the eyes.

Chloe turned her head toward Nadya as she blocked her mouth from view and questioned, "Did you know he was going to be here?"

"Of course not. Don't you think I would have mentioned that?" Nadya whispered as she stole one last glance of him before turning her head back towards her family.

He didn't see her as he seemed focused on the pasta and seafood stations.

The prickly feeling Nadya felt, rose up her spine, at the sight of him, had been unchartered territory for quite some time for her, and she wanted so badly for it not to be there because he was not available.

"Look at this stunning group of people," Dominic St. James approached the table with his arms opened wide, as he gave an invisible hug to the group.

Nadya smiled at her father, welcoming the distraction. He made his rounds and shook hands with Justin, kissed Chloe, and greeted her with a hug and a kiss on the cheek.

He took her by the hands, and had her step out so that he could take a look at her in the floor length form-fitting gown, and then pulled her back in to whisper in her ear, "I might have my Sunday best on this evening, but don't have me hurt somebody in here tonight."

Nadya tapped him on the shoulder playfully, "Oh Daddy." She smiled to herself. She could always count on her dad to make her feel like the belle of the ball.

She went to take her seat, but was halted by the appearance of her mother and the one man she never wanted to see again, although handsome in his custom tuxedo.

"Hello everyone, you all look amazing tonight. Nathan and Audrey… you guys remember Curtis from Nadya's med school days. Well, he has just accepted a surgeon position with Dom. I figured since he is new to the area, I would invite him to join us at our table tonight."

Nadine directed him to the open seat next to Nadya.

This evening was definitely starting to take a

turn for the worst as far as she was concerned. It was bad enough that he had relocated to Atlanta. Running into her ex would be inevitable.

"Nice to see you again, Nadya. You look beautiful," Curtis said, reaching out to embrace her.

"Curtis," she said curtly. Nadya allowed the hug, but stiffened in his arms. She wanted him aware that his presence was not welcomed.

She sat down, shoulders slumped in disgust.

"Nadya dear, sit-up, don't slouch in your chair," Nadine gave her a wink and kissed her husband on the cheek, before being guided to take her own seat, just as the lights dimmed and a booming voice came over the PA system.

Nadya slid up ever so slowly as strobe lights beamed in several directions, and settled as a spotlight on the steps of the staircase, illuminating a monogrammed emblem of the Surgeon's ball logo.

"Ladies and Gentleman, welcome to the 5th Annual Surgeon's Ball, Night at the Oscars. Please welcome our Mistress of Ceremony for the evening, Mrs. Nadine St. James."

Sounds of applause rang out over the large banquet hall as Nadya's mom approached the podium. She greeted the crowd and gave the purpose of the event, a rundown of the program, and a few housekeeping rules.

Nadya directed her gaze to the right toward

her mother as she spoke, not wanting to make eye contact with Curtis, although she could feel his eyes burning a hole in the back of her neck, as she looked on. Her eyes quickly grew accustomed to the darkness that blanketed the room, and she turns her head back in the direction of the galley, wishing for another glimpse of Sabien, but no such luck.

As Nadya's gaze spanned toward the front, her hazel eyes registered the presence of another fine specimen of a man, a couple of tables diagonal to hers... Banks.

He was watching her.

His tongue grazed his bottom lip ever so slightly, but enough to send shockwaves through Nadya. She turned away from him.

If her parents knew anything about their involvement, they would hit the roof. Her father would, anyway. He advised her to never get involved with anyone she worked with at the hospital.

Nadine finished her monologue of sorts and the presentation of awards began. Nadya applauded her along with the others, hoping and praying she could maintain her sanity through the evening, but it surely was not going to be easy.

Up until now Sabien had been second-guessing his decision to take this gig. His day started out with an argument with Vanessa when he dropped Serenity off. It amazed him how she could be older than him and be so immature.

When he confronted her about the absences, she simply shrugged. "It has only happened a few times," she'd said.

Then on his way to the event, he found out that his head chef was not going to make it, so he would have to cook. Then when he arrived at the venue, the woman-in-charge was perturbed upon finding out that Trish was not catering the ball. He didn't let her exasperation with him stop him from what he was there to do.

Many of the attendees recognized him from Serendipity. After shaking hands with the mayor and his wife, he walked over to the seafood and pasta stations, making sure the Alfredo sauce wasn't curdling, or the salmon wasn't drying out from the heat of the sternum below.

He turned around, and that's when he saw her. Nadya.

She was absolutely breathtaking. She was accompanied by another young woman and a guy, who he assumed was a relative due to the close resemblance. They greeted an older couple at the table with hugs and kisses before taking their seats.

Her sapphire gown glittered in the light and hugged her curves before fanning out at the bottom like a mermaid's tail. Sabien had never seen her hair in any other style but a ponytail, but this evening it was pinned up in a bundle of curls at the crown of her head, with a tendril hanging delicately down the nape of her neck.

He turned his attention back to the food, making sure everything was perfect.

When he glanced back in her direction, Nadya and her female companion seemed to be peering past him. He took one last look at the savory dishes, and walked back to the door of the galley, but did not completely disappear from sight.

With a clear view of Nadya's table, he saw a tall, salt and pepper haired gentleman, strong in stature, come over and join the group. The way he interacted with her—Sabien figured he must be Nadya's father. Soon they were joined by the condescending hostess of tonight's affair along with another gentleman.

He watched as she gave the man a hug that seemed almost intimate. Sabien felt a ping of disappointment at the thought that she could possibly be involved with someone.

"Sabien, I think we need to bring out more crab cakes."

He nodded at his crewmember in agreement.

"We have some ready. Get them from Baron."

CHAPTER 10

It was time for the Win a Dinner Date Auction. When Nadine asked Nadya to participate, it had taken a moment for her to agree. She regretted it now that Curtis was in attendance. He was here and had every opportunity to bid on a date with her.

When it was announced that the auction was about to start, Nadya excused herself, saying, "I need to freshen my make-up."

"You look fine," Chloe told her.

"No, my nose is shiny. I won't be long."

Nadya walked briskly down the mirrored hallway to the restroom.

"Please don't let Curtis bid on me," she whispered. "That is the last thing I need."

Nadya inhaled deeply and let out a relaxing

breath.

Upon exiting the ladies' room, she stopped in front of one of the gold trimmed mirrors to check out her reflection. She was glad that she had chosen this particular gown. Nadya loved the way the tiny gold speckles added a nice shimmer along with the plunging neckline. She turned to the left, lengthening her frame as she sucked in her stomach and poked out what little bit of butt she had, enhancing the fit of the dress.

"I love the way you look in dresses like this," a familiar voice hissed in her ear. She turned, meeting the lustful gaze of Wendell Banks.

"We've talked about this," she said. "We can't be seen together like this."

"We're just two colleagues passing in the wind on the way to the toilet." Wendell drew a feathery trail up the back of Nadya's arm with the tips of his fingers.

Frowning, she uttered, "Please don't touch me."

Wendell brushed aside the long ringlet of hair at the nape of her neck, and just as he was about to kiss her in that very spot, a voice came from the shadows, "I think the lady asked you to take your hands off her."

Nadya's breath caught in her throat as she recognized Sabien's voice. He stood in front of the men's restroom, arms folded.

"Guess if I win you fair and square, no one can say anything about us being in closed quarters," Wendell commented as he glared at Sabien. He walked away, apparently abandoning the idea of going to the restroom.

"How do we keep meeting up like this," she asked Sabien when it was just the two of them in the hallway.

"Forever the damsel in distress, I suppose," he said in return.

"Thanks, but you didn't have to do that. You enjoying yourself this evening?" Nadya asked, for lack of anything better to say.

"To be honest, I was actually regretting taking this gig tonight, until about two hours ago," he responded.

"And why is that?"

"Because you walked through the door."

"Flattery will get you nowhere, my dear," she said, batting her eyes. But she meant quite the contrary.

Nadya eyed her watch and noted it was just about time for the auction to begin. "I guess I'd better get back inside."

The pair walked together toward the ballroom.

Nadya stood with her back up against one wall and looked out into the crowd.

Facing her, Sabien leaned against the opposite wall, peeping out once or twice behind him to view the crowd as well.

"Nice shindig," he commented.

"Yeah, this is my mom's baby," Nadya said.

"Ahhhh, the infamous Nadine St. James. Why didn't I put it together before?" Sabien muttered almost to himself.

"I'm not sure what you mean."

"Your mother is a piece of work," he responded. "We had a bit of a run-in earlier. I don't think she was too happy about the original caterer canceling at the last minute."

"She can be rather difficult to deal with at times," Nadya acknowledged. "Imagine having to grow up with her."

They both laughed.

As if her ears were buzzing, Nadya spotted her mother sashaying over in her direction. "Nadya dear what are you doing over here by…" Her voice died when she spotted Sabien. "You'd better join the others. The auction is about to begin," Nadine eyed Sabien the entire time she was standing there.

"Mom I want to introduce you to the…"

"Yes, yes dear," Nadine interrupted, not even letting her daughter finish the introduction.

"Young man, we are in need of more champagne, and please let your boss know we will be ready for dessert as soon as the auction is over."

She headed back into the interior of the grand ballroom, without another word, but with her eyes she informed Nadya of her disdain.

"I'm so sorry about that," she apologized, embarrassed by her mother's rudeness. "Please forgive her crassness."

"Not a problem. Can't help who our parents are. Or where we get our good looks from," Sabien said.

Nadya knew he was trying his hardest not to stare too long, but she had to admit, even at fifty-nine, her mother had a very nice body. She prayed she would have the same poise and fierceness as her mom when she was her age.

"Like Mother, Like Daughter," he said, not bothering to hide his frankness. He cleared his throat. "Forgive me if I'm too forward. I just call it like I see it."

"Guess I better be going," Nadya said before heading over to the waiting area behind the stage.

"May the highest bidder win," Sabien jested.

"Ha. Be on the lookout for my bat signal, cause I might need rescuing," she said as they parted ways, both heading to their prospective areas.

Nadya made it over to the chorale just as the auctioneer began taking bids on the first bachelor. Listening to the accolades of each individual called during the auction, was impressive. It was moving quicker than she had imagined, but this year the choices were better than the past few years. There was almost twice as many participants this time as well.

She was next to last. They would be calling her name shortly.

"Now ladies and gentlemen, let us welcome Dr. Nadya St. James," the auctioneer's voice boomed over the microphone.

Nadya walked out and took her place on the stairs as all the other participants had done, as the man went through a plethora of accolades from her resume.

The blaring spotlight made it difficult to see anything but the outline of people's faces. Nadya took it upon herself to move one step down, and that was a dramatic improvement.

"One thousand dollars is the starting bid," the auctioneer said.

Nadya heard someone say, "Fifteen hundred." She forced a smile on her face because the bidder was Curtis.

The auctioneer suggested, "How about two thousand?"

Someone across the room yelled out, "Two thousand."

Then another and another, as the auction continued.

Out the corner of her eye, Nadya spied her mother coaxing Curtis. He glanced at her, his expression seemed somewhat hesitant, probably because of the scowl on her face.

The bid went up to three thousand, surprising Nadya. She hadn't expected it to be so high. What surprised her even more was when Wendell yelled out, "Thirty-five hundred."

Soon all other bids ceased and a bidding war between Curtis and Wendell ensued. Nadya was thrilled to raise so much money, but didn't like the back and forth between the two. She absolutely didn't want Curtis to win. Nadya didn't really want Wendell to win either. She knew where that date would land her. In his bed. Although she enjoyed their time together, she didn't want him becoming an addiction she couldn't afford.

"Four thousand dollars," Curtis proclaimed.

"Forty-five hundred," Wendell retorted.

Her mother was loving this. Nadya could tell from the satisfied grin on her face.

She suddenly felt like a piece of cattle, fresh on the chopping block. Nadya glanced around the room and watched heads in the audience turn back and forth between Curtis and Wendell. She stole a peek at her father who was staring at Wendell, as if trying to figure out what was really going on.

"Five thousand dollars," was Curtis's counter offer.

She had been kidding with Sabien earlier, but now her eyes traveled the room, looking for him.

"We've got five thousand," announced the auctioneer. "Going once, going twice."

Here goes nothing, Nadya thought to herself.

"*Ten thousand dollars.*"

A chorus of gasps rang out across the room and heads turned to see who had given such a hefty bid. Nadya was the only person who didn't need to see him. She broke into a grin.

"We've got ten thousand," the auctioneer announced.

A hush came over the crowd, as if everyone was waiting for another bid to come through, but there was none.

"Ten thousand going once…going twice. You have a date with the Doctor."

There stood her knight in shining armor. Chef Sabien Marshall.

Everyone applauded, including her mother.

Nadya tried not to smile too hard, but inside she was doing somersaults. Her eyes traveled to Curtis. Although she knew her mother had given him a good tongue lashing he actually looked relieved. Banks on the other hand, was visibly disappointed. He rose from his chair, adjusted his custom suit jacket and accompanying scarf, and took one glance at her before walking out.

One of the ushers held out a gloved hand to her, which she accepted, taking cautious steps down the staircase.

Before she could make her way over to Sabien, her cousin cornered her, "Giiirrllll, that man did his thang didn't he? He made a generous donation. Too bad he's married."

Sabien being married hadn't even come back into her mind, but it was indeed something to consider. "That doesn't mean a thing. All good business owners, have a certain amount of money they plan to invest in various charities over the course of the year," she said, attempting to shut the notion down before she allowed her brain to go there.

"Whatever the reason, at least you know you will have some good food," Chloe commented, before heading back over to Justin.

As she looked across the room, Nadya no longer saw Sabien standing near the auction officials and had no idea where he was. Then she felt a tap on her shoulder, and turned to find him standing there with his chef's coat draped over his arm.

"Thanks for the save... again," Nadya said with gratitude.

"You looked like you could use a little rescuing," he replied with a bow, then rewarded her with the most gorgeous smile.

The smoldering look in his brown eyes made her completely forget about her apprehension about him being married, as she anticipated the dinner.

CHAPTER II

Sunday morning came with no warning.

When the sound of her mother's ringtone consumed the quietness of her bedroom, Nadya covered her head with her pillow.

She thought she had escaped until the ringing started again. It was no use ignoring her. Nadine would just keep calling until she picked up. She reached over to the nightstand to retrieve her phone and held it up to her ear.

"Wake up. Have you seen the morning paper?"

Umm, no Mom. You just told me to wake up so how could I have seen the paper? Nadya wanted to say, but knew better.

"I'm still in bed."

"You and Chef Boyardee, made the front page," she stated frankly.

Nadya sprang up in her bed, all thoughts of sleep evaporated.

"We what?"

"Front page of the AJC," her mother stated.

Nadya leaped out of bed, almost tripping over the tangled bed sheets. After freeing herself, she stepped into her slippers and rushed to open the front door. Phone in hand, she ran out to grab the newspaper from the lawn. The frigid February air slapped her in the face and surged through the thin material of her pajamas.

She reached down in the crunchy, ice covered grass, picked up the newspaper, then rushed back into her warm house. She was about to lay her cell phone on the banister, when she heard her mother calling her name. Nadya had forgotten she was still on the line.

"Sorry Mom," she apologized.

"Goodness Nadya, if I hadn't heard the scuffling in the phone, I would have thought you hung up on me," Nadine said.

"Hold on Mom, I'm opening the newspaper now." Nadya pulled the newspaper from the wet plastic, dropping it momentarily to the tiled floor of her kitchen.

She unrolled it, and sure enough, there in the flesh, on the front page, was a picture of her and Sabien. He was bent in a bow and she was standing before him with her hands clasped in front of her and the caption read: ***Auction at the Surgeon's Ball Brings a True Prince Charming to the Princess.***

"Mom, you there?" Nadya checked for breathing on the other end of the phone.

"Yeeesss. It took you long enough. Please explain to me why I wasn't told that he was *the* Sabien Marshall. I thought he was just one of the help—not the owner of Serendipity. Did you know that?"

"Yes Mom, I did and I tried to tell you. If you hadn't been so rude last night when I tried to introduce the two of you—you probably would have found out who he was."

"Don't get snippy with me young lady. I'm still your mother."

"You are too funny Mom. Listen, can I go back to sleep now? I will call you later." Nadya hung up the phone with her mother.

She put the cellphone down on the kitchen table, paused once more to admire the photo of them in the newspaper, which was now sprawled out on the table in front of her.

Nadya yawned. "Definitely need a few more Zzzs."

She navigated back to her bedroom and back in the comfort of her bed.

CHAPTER 12

It was not very often that Sabien had to jump in and lend a helping hand in the "pit," a nickname he gave his kitchen because the quick and robotic flow of the staff, reminded him of the fast paced motion of the pit crew at a NASCAR race.

Today, however, was one of those days.

A quick glance at the clock on the wall revealed the dinner hour was just getting started at a quarter past six. With a lengthy reservation list, including several large parties for bachelorette parties, convention attendees, and sports teams, Serendipity was buzzing with patrons already—not to mention the nice plug he received from catering the Surgeon's Benefit Ball.

Another bonus to catering the ball, was the

fact that he'd won a date with the beautiful Dr. St. James. The whole situation was still rather ironic to him. He was baffled by the fact that Nadya was the daughter of the host of the event and one of the most prominent African American couples in the area.

He was sure by the look Mrs. St. James gave him, that she was shocked when he won the bid for her daughter. She was clearly not pleased, but she was thrilled with the nice check he wrote out to the organization. Sabien had not yet reached out to Nadya. They had exchanged numbers at the end of the night, but when he didn't hear from her, he figured she was one of those girls who didn't make the first move.

Pots and pans clanged against the iron burner grates on the stove tops and the sharp, serrated edges of the kitchen knives chop meats and vegetables on cutting boards, in preparation for all the various entrées to be served. Sabien, satisfied with the pace at which things were moving, edged his way out of the kitchen and over to the hostess station to see how things were going.

"How are we looking over here, Kat?" he asked his head hostess.

"So far so good chief," she responded, marking an X across a square on the seating placard.

"That's what I like to hear." Sabien turned to

greet a new set of customers who have just arrived, and felt the vibration of his cellphone in his pants pocket. Checking the screen, he noted the name of Serenity's school.

He answered making his way to the door to step outside, "Hello."

"Hello, Mr. Marshall. This is Mrs. Darzi at Mahatma Academy. I am calling because Ms. Marshall has yet to pick up Serenity, and it's an half hour past our closing time. Could you please come and get her?"

Sabien had barely digested her words, but was already seeing fire. He rubbed his hand over his head, and grabbed on to the back of his neck.

"Yes of course, I will be right there to pick her up." Sabien said goodbye and hung up the phone. He was furious. Things had been going seemingly well, since he'd given Vanessa a stern talking to in regards to the previous incidents that had transpired at Serenity's school.

She kept saying Serenity had been sick and that's why she hadn't been at school, and promised profusely that she would not be late again picking her up. *Where could she be?*

Sabien rushed back inside to inform his management team that he had to step out but would be back as soon as he could. It was a good thing, his crew ran his operation like a well-oiled machine and really didn't need much direction from him.

Sabien hopped in his car and sped off towards the school.

When he arrived, he caught sight of Serenity through the floor length glass windows at the entrance, sitting on a bench twiddling her thumbs. It was a gut-wrenching moment for him, because even though he would never think Mrs. Darzi or any of the other staff would leave her there alone, he thought of all the what ifs and wanted to tear into Vanessa.

Sabien didn't bother parking properly in a parking space because there were no other cars in the parking lot. As he entered through the front door, Serenity looked up and ran to him.

"Daaaaaddddyy," she called out to him.

He swiftly lifted her up into his arms, and hugged her tightly, just as Mrs. Darzi appeared in the doorway of her office, prepared to leave. She looked irritated and he couldn't blame her. Having to stay late on a Friday because a parent forgot to pick up their child was enough to anger anyone.

She greeted him coolly. "Mr. Marshall. Sorry I had to bother you with this."

"No apology needed, Mrs. Darzi. I'm so sorry you were inconvenienced in such a manner." He grabbed Serenity's backpack from the floor next to the bench and they headed to the car.

"Daddy, where's Mommy? I want to go home," Serenity questioned, her voice barely above a whisper as she laid her head on her daddy's shoulder.

"I don't know Reese Cup, but we're going to find out.

By the time Sabien reached Vanessa's, it was 7:30 p.m. and he was pissed.

Sabien pulled into the driveway as he had done so many times over the years, and immediately saw Vanessa's silver Mercedes in its normal spot.

He swiftly unhooked Serenity's seatbelt and she ran up to the front door, hastily leaving her belongings behind. Sabien was a few steps behind her, after grabbing her backpack, and just as she went to knock on the door, it opened and Vanessa stepped out, all geared up to go somewhere, with her purse and keys in hand.

At the sight of Sabien and Serenity, she stopped dead in her tracks.

"Oh my goodness Serenity, I have been calling the school for the past hour and no one's been answering."

"You can't be serious right now, Vanessa," Sabien uttered.

"I'm sorry, Sabien. I got home early from the school and thought I would lay down and take a nap, and I must've overslept."

"Last time I checked, I left here with plenty of

clocks so that's no excuse."

"I have been having major issues with sleeping, so I had Dr. Stansfield prescribe me something. I guess I didn't take it early enough for it to take effect, and me still be able to get up and function properly."

Sabien looked at her dumbfounded, "If I didn't have one of the craziest nights at the spot tonight, I would take her with me." He stooped down to his daughter's level and said, "Hey Reese Cup. Do you remember Daddy's phone number?"

"404-556-3122," Serenity rambled the number off to him with no hesitation.

"Yes. Daddy is so proud of you. Call me if you need me?"

"Ok," Serenity said, hugging him tightly around the neck.

Vanessa grabbed her hand to take her daughter inside.

Just as she was about to close the door, Sabien pressed a hand up against the door to stop her, "You better drink some chamomile tea, count some sheep or something. I'm not trying to hear that you are doped up while Serenity is with you. What if something bad happens? Are you sure you're lucid enough to watch her now?"

"Nothing's going to happen, Sabien. I've got this under control."

"Some control," Sabien commented as he headed to his car.

Before he took the first step he heard Vanessa talking to Serenity, "You hungry, baby? Mommy has some fresh cookies and milk?"

"They won't make my tummy hurt this time, will they?"

"No of course not," Vanessa reassured her and closed the door.

Sabien hustled back to his car and dashed back to the restaurant.

CHAPTER 13

"So Nadya darling, I assume you haven't been on your date yet with Mr. Marshall."

"No Mom…" Nadya responded in a sing-song voice.

"Naddi, leave the girl alone, and let her eat her food in peace," Dominic St. James said in his daughter's defense, with a loving wink in her direction.

Nadya smiled. Her daddy always came through.

"Oh hush, Dom. I got confirmation that we received his generous donation, so I was just checking to see if Nadya had honored her end of the deal," Nadine clarified before taking a sip of her red wine.

"Thanks Mom. Way to make me feel like a piece of meat."

"Nonsense dear. I just know if Curtis would have won the bid, you would have been on numerous dates by now," she said with a smug grin.

Nadya's father eyed his daughter shaking his head, as he moved his attention back to his plate.

"Well, I guess Curtis couldn't roll with the big dogs that night, allowing himself to be outbid and all. But then again, he is one for getting out before things get too heavy for him."

"Oh Nadya, you guys were young, and pursuing your medical careers. Things happen, but there's always a chance to reconcile. I have his number if you want to reach out to him, although I'm sure you will be seeing plenty of him soon enough."

When hell freezes over, Nadya thought to herself. She had never shared the real details of what happened with her and Curtis, and she had no intentions of doing so now.

"See, I knew you put him up to that. All of it," Nadya uttered.

"What on earth do you mean, sweetheart?" Her mom asked with a baffled expression on her face.

"Mom don't give me that. You are always trying to play the matchmaker. Just give it up. If I get one more random voicemail from someone you met at a political forum or a philanthropic event, I'm going to kill myself." Nadya pointed her finger down her throat in a gagging motion, prompting laughter from her father.

"Stop being so melodramatic," her mom retorted, giving her husband the evil eye.

"Long-term relationships aren't for me, and I'm ok with that. I wish you could get there as well."

"As long as I have breath in my body, I will make it my life's goal to see you married to someone who can provide for you," Nadine said.

"Justin may be a regular run of the mill guy, but he seems to be able to provide for Chloe," Nadya responded.

"No daughter of mine is gonna be backed into a corner," Dominic interjected. "That is why we raised her to be self-sufficient, a go-getter, an over-achiever. So she wouldn't have to ride on the shirt tails of any man."

The color drained from Nadine's café au lait skin.

Dominic apparently hit a sore spot because her mother tossed her cloth napkin onto her plate and retreated to the living room.

Her father raised his eyebrows in Nadya's direction. "I guess I better go talk my way out of the dog house."

Nadya poked at her food. She really wished her mother would just leave her love life alone.

An image of Sabien crossed her mind, including the tattooed ring on his finger. She was grateful that he had played Robin Hood to her Maid Marion during the auction.

Nadya poked a little while longer at the food on her plate, and then pushed it forward and placed her knife and fork on top in a crisscrossed fashion, and made haste in getting the kitchen back in order. She had an early appointment in the morning and really needed to get home to bed. Her parents cleaning lady wasn't due until Thursday, and Nadya knew her mother would not rest if her kitchen wasn't spotless.

As she rinsed the dishes and placed them neatly in the dishwasher, she heard the sound of her mother and father's laughter, which warmed her heart. Nadya never liked when her parents were upset with one another. Aside from Chloe's parents, her mother and father were the only true example she's had for relationships that withstand the test of time. Their shining example of love was the one true constant in her life. It was proof that true love really existed.

CHAPTER 14

Nadya arrived bright and early at her practice the next day, and was greeted by her receptionist who met her at the door with a toasted bagel and a Cinnamon Dolce Latte from Starbucks®.

"Thank you, Simone. You're the best."

"No problem, boss lady. Oh and there is a package for you in your office. It came yesterday, just as we were locking up for the evening."

Nadya was greeted by the fragrant scent of flowers.

An assortment of pink, white, and orange Stargazer lilies in a beautiful crystal vase with an intricate design etched into it, sat on her desk.

They were her favorite flowers.

She leaned over the bouquet and took in the

perfumed aroma through her nostrils. She reached in the middle of the bouquet to grab the small white envelope addressed to her. Freeing the tiny card from its holder, she read it:

Hoping you will honor your commitment

and join me for dinner

March 27th @ 7pm

Serendipity

~SRM

RSVP: You know where to reach me

For a split second, she was overwhelmed with a giddy feeling, at the prospect of their date, but she toned it down. He was a married man, for one. And second, this wasn't a real date. He had been the highest bidder for charity.

Nadya re-attached the card and envelope back to the plastic clip, and inhaled one last time before she headed out of her office to see her first patient of the day.

Time passed quickly. Before she realized it, Nadya was signing off on the chart of her sixth patient.

"Serenity Marshall is in exam room number four Dr. St. James," her nurse informed her.

Surprised, Nadya asked, "Do you know what

she's here for today? Her name wasn't on the appointments list."

"Something about headaches," the woman confirmed before heading in the direction of the nurse's station.

Nadya rounded the corner to access room number four. She expected to see Sabien, but was greeted by Serenity and her mother. The little girl was sitting on the bench next to Vanessa with her head laying in her mother's lap.

"Hi, Dr. Nadya," Serenity spoke with a muffled voice as her mom continued to rub her head.

"So what seems to bring you here today?"

"She started complaining of a headache a couple days ago, and it's gotten progressively worse, so I wanted to bring her in."

"No Mommy, it doesn't hurt anymore."

"Serenity Reese, stop trying to sit up before you make it worse."

"Has she been doing anything out of the ordinary that would have caused her head to hurt?"

"Not to my knowledge, I was thinking it was a viral infection of some kind. Ear infection maybe."

"Let's have a look shall we?" Nadya patted on the bed with her hand, and Serenity hopped up on the bed to take a seat. She examined her nose, eyes, ears, and throat and noted that everything was clear there.

"I don't see any signs of infection in any of the key areas. Is she getting enough sleep? Has she ever had her vision checked because it could be related to that? I know it's rather early for this to be done in her case because it's not usually assessed until around the age of five."

"No she hasn't," Vanessa confirmed, "but I really think there's an infection somewhere."

Nadya couldn't figure out why Vanessa was so sure there was something wrong with her child. Most parents were elated when they found their children free from illness. Not this one. She actually looked disappointed.

"At this point, since there's nothing to confirm where the headaches are coming from, I advise to give her Children's Tylenol or generic acetaminophen."

"Thank you, Dr. St. James. I just didn't want her to go back to school in pain," Vanessa said, a look of apprehension on her face.

"If the headaches persist, please don't hesitate to reach out to me," Nadya said handing the discharge papers to Vanessa, as she watched Serenity hop back and forth between the four colored squares on the exam room floor. *Doesn't look someone with a headache to me.* She made a mental note to follow-up on the little girl's medical records from her previous doctors. Something just didn't add up.

"Serenity sweet pea, let's go. We gotta get you to school before they call the law looking for you."

Nadya gave her a questioning look, and Vanessa laughed nervously.

They walked out of the room together and up the hall towards the checkout area. Before they reached the window, they passed Nadya's office.

"What a beautiful arrangement. Serenity's father used to give those to me all the time."

Her words dampened Nadya's elation over the flowers. Sabien could have been just a little more original.

"Those look like the flowers me and Daddy picked out yesterday," Serenity announced. Both she and Vanessa glanced down at the little girl, and then at each other.

"Bye, Dr. Nadya," Serenity called, pulling her out of her trance.

Saved by the bell.

"Bye Serenity. Take care,"

Nadya walked back to her office and took a seat behind her desk. She eyed the card attached to the flowers once more. She knew what she had to do.

Sabien was a married man and although their dinner was one for charity—Nadya wanted nothing to do with a potential scandal.

She waited until the end of the day to call him. Nadya pulled out his business card, dialed the number and waited for him to answer.

"Sabien Marshall speaking."

"It's Nadya. I'm calling to let you off the hook. You don't have to take me to dinner."

"May I ask why?"

"You're married and I'm your daughter's doctor—I just think it would be too awkward."

"I'm no longer married, Nadya. Vanessa and I are divorced."

"Oh..." she murmured. Inside, her heart leapt with joy. She didn't have to feel guilty for fantasizing about him.

"I hope we can still have our dinner," Sabien said. "I created a menu just for you."

She smiled. "I'm actually looking forward to it."

CHAPTER 15

Nadya arrived at Serendipity promptly at seven p.m. on Tuesday, two weeks later.

She was surprised to find the parking lot so vacant. There were a few cars parked there, but the last time she was there with Chloe—there was hardly an empty space available.

Maybe something had come up and Sabien had to close the restaurant.

Nadya checked her phone to see if he had texted or left her a voice message.

Nothing.

She was about to leave when the door opened and Sabien stepped outside.

"Welcome. I thought you were going to sit in the parking lot all night," he commented when she approached him.

Nadya's eyes traveled around the restaurant, looking for signs of life.

As if reading her mind, Sabien told her, "They are finishing up some duties and will be out of here shortly. Then you have me all to yourself."

"I was not expecting this at all."

"What? You've never had a guy shut down his establishment for you, for a first date?"

"No, I have not."

"Nice to know I am your first," he said and when she looked up at him, he winked at her.

The gesture thrilled her.

Sabien escorted Nadya to a well-appointed table. He pulled out a chair for her to sit down.

She admired the table arrangement including the stargazers that adorned each of the plates at the center of the place setting. "This is beautiful."

"I'm glad you like it," he responded. "I hope you're hungry."

On the table was a nice selection of pastries and fruit.

Sabien strolled over to the bar, quickly returning with two Champagne glasses filled with a bubbly orange concoction anchored by orange halves.

Mimosas.

He sat down across from her and lifted the bread basket offering her a scone.

After he blessed the food, Nadya pinched off

a piece. "Mmmmm." The dough melted in her mouth.

"We aim to please," he said, smiling. "Is there any fruit you are allergic to or don't like?"

She shook her head.

He placed a few pieces from the colorful assortment onto her plate.

"Thank you," she said and they ate in silence for a moment.

Just as they finished their first course, a uniformed person rolled out a table with a humongous platter on it. All the dishes were covered, but she knew whatever was underneath, would be amazing.

"Nadya meet my head chef, Chris."

He took her hand in his and kissed it.

"Ever the charmer. Get outta here," Sabien joked with Chris and hit him on his back with the cloth napkin he'd had in his lap.

"So did you save room for the main course?"

Nadya's cheeks burned of embarrassment as she eyed her empty plate.

"It's ok. I love a woman with a good palette for great food," he looked her way with another wink and her heart skipped a beat. Sabien proceeded to remove the covers from each dish. Nadya was in awe of the smorgasbord he'd planned for the evening. Her stomach growled in agreement and she blushed.

"So did you make your staff stay here to cook all this up for you, and now you're sending them home?"

He smiled that incredible smile she couldn't seem to get enough of, "As a matter of fact, I prepared everything you see before you."

"Really? I'm impressed." Nadya was touched that he'd done this for her. It was very thoughtful.

"I really couldn't figure out what to make for you," he confessed, "but a little birdie reminded me that you love breakfast food. That being said, I just cooked up a few of my favorites—so you have options. Plus, I wasn't sure if you ate pork, beef, turkey or any meat at all." He paused a moment before saying, "In the center, we have the vegetarian scramble with broccoli, mushrooms, onions, peppers and egg whites, topped with cheddar cheese. The dish next to that has an assortment of meats, then there's French toast, Old Fashioned Potato cakes, and grits."

As he pointed out each dish, Nadya hung on to his every word, but she would be lying if she said she wasn't ready to dig in. She wanted to savor every morsel.

They engaged each other with small talk during their meal.

She settled back in her chair. "So speaking of

a little birdie, was Serenity with you when you bought those flowers for me?"

He finished the bite of food he had in his mouth and answered, "Yes, she was with me."

"She mentioned it to her mother during her last doctor's visit."

From the expression on his face, she guessed he was caught off guard. "I'm sorry, did I say something wrong," she asked as he pulled his cell phone out of his pocket and scrolled down on his screen.

"No, not at all. I didn't have that appointment on my calendar. I don't know how I missed it."

"It wasn't a scheduled appointment. Your ex-wife brought her in because she had a headache. I didn't find anything wrong with her." Nadya eyed Sabien. "If you don't mind my asking... how long have you been divorced?"

"Six months," he responded. "We share joint custody of Serenity." Sabien took a sip of his Mimosa. "Now tell me something about you. Age? Only Child? Credit Score? Criminal History?" he rolled out a litany of questions.

Nadya burst into laughter. "Somebody wasn't prepared, were they?"

"Just like to know what I'm getting myself into," he retorted.

"Ok let's see. I'm thirty-five. Yes. I can hold my own, and I've never killed anyone."

Sabien chuckled.

Laughter was easy to come by with him, and she liked this.

"Oh yeah, and what's the deal with the two guys at the ball? They were really vying for you during the auction."

Nadya knew the question might come, but she wasn't really in the mood to discuss her tumultuous past with Curtis. And how could she explain the thing she had going on with Banks? It was definitely not appropriate conversation for a first date.

"Curtis is an ex-boyfriend from medical school. As for Banks, well… we work together." She arched her eye in his direction, expecting him to press more, but he didn't and she was glad.

"So, no kids for you?" Sabien inquired.

She knew that question was in there, though it was a tough subject for her. "No kids… I need to visit the restroom," Nadya said, quickly changing the subject, and needing a minute to regroup. Sabien pointed her in the direction of the restroom.

She walked out expecting to find Sabien where she left him, but instead she noted that the dishes were now cleared and the tables were spread out to open up the dance floor. She also heard the faint sound of Joe playing over the sound system.

"May I have this dance?" Sabien whispered from behind.

Nadya turned around to oblige him.

They danced in silence, both taking in the ambiance of the moment. They started out at arm's-length, but as their gazes deepened and their comfort levels rose, Nadya felt his arms envelop her, pulling her closer to him until their bodies touched.

Nadya wrapped her arms around his neck and allowed her mind to be carried off into a different dimension, where all that mattered was him and her in that moment. They remained like that as the tracks changed over and over again. When the music finally stopped, they had no choice but to come back to reality.

"The previous conversation was a little heavy for first date. So tell me something about you that I wouldn't know just from looking at you," he said as he led her to a cozy corner in front of a velvet curtain, with sofas and arm chairs.

They sat down on a loveseat.

Sabien reached in front of them to a table already occupied with an ice bucket filled with a bottle of wine along with two wine glasses. He popped the cork, filling them halfway, then handed one to her.

"Thank you," she said. It was tasty, and not too dry. Just how she liked it. "You wouldn't know that I play the piano."

"Oh really? So how about you play something for me?"

"I would, but I don't see a piano in here." Her gaze spanned the small area with her eyes.

Sabien pulled the velvet curtain back, revealing a small stage with microphone, a saxophone stand, and a piano.

"Guess, I'm in luck," he said. "We have live music every now and then."

He rose to his feet.

Sabien pulled out the bench and gestured for her to take a seat.

Nadya took a deep breath, and closed her eyes while her fingers familiarized themselves with the keys. It wasn't long before she had delved into her own rendition of Stevie Wonder's *Ribbon in the Sky*. Not realizing she had been so enraptured in the song with her eyes closed the whole time, she opened them and found Sabien standing inches away.

There were no words but as her nose took in the woody smell of his cologne that she'd grown to love over the small amount of time they had known each other, he leaned in to kiss her, and she doesn't deny him. It wasn't an intense kiss, but light and delicate. A really nice way for their lips to be introduced to one another. Her hand rose to touch the light stubble that etched his face.

"Forgive me for being so forward," Sabien said softly as they slowly released their lips to gaze again into one another's eyes.

"No forgiveness necessary. It was nice," Nadya replied. She leaned forward to kiss him again, this time on the cheek, but yawned before she could get there.

"Am I keeping someone out past their bedtime?"

She looked at her watch, noting that it was now a quarter to eleven, "If I'm not working, I am usually in the bed by now. I'm an early riser so I gotta make sure I get my beauty rest."

Sabien moved a tendril of hair behind her ear, "No rest needed. I'm sure it comes naturally."

She laughed, "You are some smooth talker."

"Yeah, well this smooth talker is going to be a gentleman and let you get home." Sabien grabbed her hand to help her stand and move behind the piano bench. They pushed it underneath the piano together, and pulled the velvet curtain down in front of it.

At the car, he kissed her one more time, "I hope you had a nice time tonight."

"I did. I hope the evening was worth every bit of your ten thousand."

"Being able to donate money to charity was just the icing on the cake."

Nadya got into her car and Sabien closed the door behind her. She rolled down the window and winked.

As she pulled out of the parking lot, she saw his silhouette in the darkness, and thought about how much she really liked this man. No matter how hard she tried to keep her emotions at bay, being around him prompted her to reconsider her view on relationships.

The following day, Nadya stopped by the restaurant to see Sabien.

"Hello there," he said, greeting her with a hug. Serenity was eating a bowl of macaroni and cheese.

"Hello Mr. Marshall," she flirted as she returned the hug. The warmth of her body was a welcomed treat, and reminded him of their first dance last week.

"Hi Dr. Nadya, would you like some mac and cheese? Chris has plenty left to share."

Sabien and Nadya laughed in unison at Serenity's emphasis on the fact that there was more in the kitchen, as if to say she would not be sharing hers.

"I can't stay long, but I wanted to say thank you for last night. It was wonderful."

"So miss ladybug what are you up to," Nadya stroked Serenity's curly hair.

"Mommy's throwing me a party for my birthday, can you come?"

"I don't know sweetie. I think that's probably only for family," Nadya replied.

Serenity shook her head. "No it's not. My friends will be there and they're not family."

"She definitely has a point there," Sabien said with a grin.

Nadya was pretty sure that Vanessa wouldn't be happy with her showing up. "Tell you what. How about you tell me what you want. I can still get you a birthday gift even if I can make it to the party."

"I really want an American Girl Doll. The one that looks like me," Serenity said.

"An American girl doll that looks like Serenity. *Got it*." She pretended to write it on her hand with her finger as a pencil.

Her gaze traveled to Sabien. "I gotta run. Going to meet up with Chloe for some more wedding stuff. Call me." She motioned with her hand held up to her ear like a makeshift phone.

Sabien nodded. "You can count on it."

"Take care of Daddy, Serenity," she called over her shoulder as she walked out.

***

"Daddy, I like Dr. Nadya. Is she going to be my new mommy?" Serenity asked.

"Baby, you only have one Mommy." *No matter how temperamental.*

He liked Nadya as well. She was like a breath of fresh air for him—something he hadn't experienced in a long time. Sabien felt like fate had drawn them together and he didn't plan to let Nadya get away.

Chapter 16

"I'm glad you could make it." The sound of Sabien's voice always had a mesmerizing effect on her. Her legs were like Jell-O under the weight of her body, but she remained steady.

He invited her to Serendipity for his daughter's fifth birthday party. "I was surprised to get your call this morning. Are you sure it's okay for me to be here?"

"Of course. This is my restaurant and you're Serenity's doctor. She really wanted you to be here." He paused a moment before adding, "So did I."

"Where can I put this?" she asked, holding up a colorful gift bag.

"Right this way," Sabien swung his arms to the left with a slight bow and pointed her in the direction of the cake and gift table. She couldn't help but notice his signature dark denim jeans and black V-neck shirt. It was a simple ensemble, but always set off fireworks within her when she saw him, especially because it offered a more defined view of his athletic build, which she couldn't help but to admire.

Once they made their way to the party area, Nadya was greeted by a petite woman with white roller-set hair and glasses, who she knew right away had to be the aunt Sabien had mentioned during one of their phone conversations.

"Aw, you must be *the* Dr. Nadya. My baby talks about you all of the time. Come over here and give me a big hug," she said with outstretched arms.

Nadya obliged. "You must be *the* Aunt Cori."

The warmth of the woman's body and the scent of roses, along with her snug embrace consumed her. Nadya felt like she'd known the woman her whole life.

"So nice to meet you. I hope Serenity didn't have too many bad things to say about me."

"Serenity had plenty to say, but that's not the baby I was talking about." She gave a slight nod in Sabien's direction.

"Come on Aunt Cori, really?" he said with a look of embarrassment.

It thrilled her knowing that she'd been on his

mind as much as he'd been on hers.

"Oh hush boy, that's the problem with you youngsters these days," Cori fussed. "Always trying to play hard to get. That's how the good ones get away. You better make it plain, and scoop this fine young lady up. I'm sure she has plenty of other's knocking down her door for a chance."

Nadya felt her face heat up.

He gave Nadya an apologetic stare, and she smiled at him. Even if she didn't say it out loud, she wanted him to know that she didn't take any offense to his aunt's comments. She appreciated her candidness, and wished she was carefree enough to tell him how she felt about him.

Serenity and her friends danced around the room to the popular tunes coming from the speakers. The little girl looked like she was having a great time.

"Where's Vanessa?"

A scowl briefly consumed his handsome face, and Nadya immediately wished she could take her question back.

Aunt Cori noted Sabien's expression, "Don't mind him sweetheart." She leaned over to Nadya, placing her hand to the side of her mouth, as if shielding her words from earshot, but does not lower her voice, so Sabien was still able to hear. "I don't know if he told you or not, but that ex-wife of his supposedly had this big shindig planned for Serenity's birthday last Saturday, but the night before Sabien called to see if she needed help with anything--she acted as though she had no idea what he was talking about. Come to find out, she didn't have a thing planned. Hadn't even reserved a location." Aunt Cori shook her head.

Nadya saw a flash of anger in Sabien's eyes. From the sound of it, he had every right to be upset.

"You're a doctor. Can't you prescribe something for her?"

"*Aunt Cori*. Enough already. Besides Nadya is not that kind of doctor. She's a pediatrician."

"Listen, I'm going to go make sure the pasta and breadsticks are ready in the back and then we will get started. You good? Want something to drink?"

"I'm fine. Do you need help with anything?"

"Just enjoy the party," Sabien responded, giving her a bit of a smile. He walked through the double doors that led into the kitchen.

Nadya took a seat at the table across from Aunt Cori.

"Please tell me I didn't offend you."

"Oh no, of course not," Nadya responded.

"I just hate to see my boy go through so many changes with that woman. Ever since they lost their son, she has never been the same. I never really liked the way she hooked her claws into Sabien while he was under her tutelage."

Nadya interjected, "He was her student?"

"Yup. They met when he attended *Le Cordon Bleu* in Paris. The day they called to tell me they were getting married, I had a fit, but after a while—I saw they genuinely loved each other. Then we lost Jeremiah when he was just six months old, and she was never the same."

"If you don't mind me asking. What happened?" Nadya asked.

"SIDS," Cori stated. "After Serenity was born, I thought things were back on track, but that was short-lived as her personality shifted. She has what I believe is a jealous spirit towards Serenity's relationship with Sabien."

Nadya was surprised. "How could she be jealous of her own child?"

"I have no idea, but there's something going on with Vanessa."

Cori had given Nadya an unexpected earful, especially considering they had just met. She and Sabien hadn't even gotten into this much detail about his relationship with Vanessa.

"Doctor Nadya. You *came.*" Serenity rushed over to the table and hugged Nadya's legs as her friends tagged close behind.

"Hey little lady. I am lovin' this outfit. Do you guys think I could find a tutu in my size to wear?"

"Nooo…" the little girl chorus sang in unison.

Nadya and Cori laughed.

Sabien made his way over with a piping hot chafing dish filled to the brim with Fettuccini Alfredo. A member of his wait staff came over with two bowls; one with shrimp and the other sautéed chicken, along with breadsticks.

The girls took a seat at the party table, decorated with a Doc McStuffins theme.

The music stopped just as Sabien worked to divvy out the entrée, and Nadya jumped in behind him, passing out the garlic bread.

Suddenly, there was a loud thud coming from the direction of the hostess stand. Everyone's eyes turned in the direction of the noise, and found Vanessa standing next to a table not too far away.

The strings of a bouquet of balloons dangled from her mouth, purse in hand, and a cardboard box full of wrapped gifts now on the table.

She removed the tangled strings from her mouth, "Looks like I made it just in time." She scanned the party scene, and her glaring eyes landed on Nadya in disgust.

Nadya dropped the last piece of garlic bread back onto the tray with the serving tongs, and sat the tray on the table. Serenity removed her cloth napkin from her lap and immediately ran to her mother.

"Mommyy…" Serenity dashed over to her mother.

Vanessa quickly placed the weighted balloons on the table and scooped her daughter up into a bear hug. "Hi baby, you didn't think I was going to miss your party did you?"

"What'd you bring me? Huh?" Serenity asked with excitement in her voice.

"All kinds of surprises, and there are more in the car, and gift bags for your friends too." Vanessa replied.

Out of the corner of her eye, Nadya saw Cori roll her eyes. It was obvious that she was trying to overcompensate for screwing up the original birthday plans.

Sabien walked over to Vanessa and offered assistance with the items she'd brought with her, while Nadya worked to reel her emotions in.

How dare she show up like this after Sabien had to pick up the pieces from the mess she had made of Serenity's birthday celebration, trying to outdo him. Nadya knew she was being overly agitated for someone who didn't really have a say so. But what if she and Sabien decided to pursue something more, would things always be this way? *More than likely, yes*, she told herself.

Sabien and Vanessa both walked over to the table, Serenity still comfortably affixed to her mother's hip.

"Hi Aunt Cori," Vanessa greeted.

"Vanessa," she retorted with not so much as a look in her direction, as she spun the noodles on her plate around her fork.

Vanessa placed Serenity down in her seat and took a seat next to her daughter.

"Mighty cozy aren't we, Dr. St. James?"

"Vanessa, would you like something to eat?" Sabien asked.

"Of course, sweetheart. You know your Alfredo is one of my favorites," she gushed trying a hand at jealousy tactics as she placed her purse on the corner of the table next to Serenity.

Sabien ignored her comment and grabbed another plate to scoop a hearty portion onto it before passing it to her. "Did you tell Dr. St. James, how we came up with your special sauce during one of our sexcapades in Paris" Vanessa continued, trying her best to get a rise out of him, or maybe it was aimed at her. Nadya thought the latter, and moved to get up, but Cori pressed a hand on her leg underneath the table to keep her in place. Arms folded, she settled back into her seat, and peered in her direction.

"Vanessa." Sabien's stern tone is evidence of his

aggravation.

"*What?* It's the truth. I just think DOCTOR St. James, should hear a different side of your history lesson. We loved as passionately as we argued."

Vanessa turned to Serenity and asked, "So, baby, have you been taking your allergy medicine?"

What allergy medicine? she wondered. There was nothing noted in the little girl's file. Nadya made a mental note to ask Sabien.

"No, Daddy said I don't need it." Serenity answered through a mouth of full of pasta.

"Serenity, don't talk with your mouth full," Sabien chastised her.

"What do you mean, she doesn't need it? Sabien, I told you when you picked her up that she had been sneezing a lot and had watery eyes,"

"That very well may have been the case, but she didn't experience any of that with me, and I'm not gonna give my child medicine just for the heck of it," he replied. "She's never needed allergy medicine before."

"So how do you explain the nosebleeds?" Vanessa snapped at him.

When he doesn't have a quick come back, Nadya spoke up,

"Allergy medications contain antihistamines that can cause the nose to dry out, and thus cause nosebleeds, if the nose is not lubricated sufficiently."

"Where do you get off telling me how to treat my child?" Vanessa snapped.

"I'm your child's pediatrician," Nadya's statement shut her down briefly.

"Not for long," Vanessa responded in a low tone, but loud enough for Serenity to hear. She began to cry.

"Noooo Daddy, you said I wouldn't have to change doctors anymore. You promised," she whined through big crocodile tears.

Vanessa's voice grew maniacal over the cries of her daughter.

Sabien rose from his chair and walked around to Vanessa, taking a tight grip of her arm, and pulled her up from her seat and led her somewhere to talk privately.

Serenity was inconsolable. Her arms were slumped down onto the table, but not before she knocked Vanessa's purse tumbling to the floor with all its contents spilled out haphazardly.

"Oh no. Oh no. Mommy's gonna be so mad," Serenity cried even harder than before.

Before she knew what hit her, Nadya rushed to her aid, "Serenity baby, it's ok. Mommy's not gonna be mad. It was just an accident. How about I help you pick everything up before she gets back, and it will be like nothing ever happened. Then you can get back to partying." Nadya did her best to console the little girl.

She grabbed one of the cloth napkins to dab at Serenity's eyes.

"Come on girls, let's go see if we can get Chris to put in another CD, it's mighty quiet in here," Aunt Cori placed her arms around two little girls, who seemed confused by what has transpired.

Nadya assisted Serenity with gathering the displaced items and putting them back into

Vanessa' purse.

"You are much too pretty to cry at your own birthday party. Don't you know that?"

Serenity nodded and smiled, and the twinkle in her almond-shaped eyes was soon rekindled.

Just as they deposited what they thought was the last item, Serenity turned her head to look under the table, "Hey wait, we forgot something." She reached underneath the table and retrieved a pill bottle and handed it to Nadya.

Before Nadya placed it back in the purse, she read the label: *Lithium carbonate, 600 mg in the morning, afternoon, and nighttime for the treatment of manic depression.*

Nadya made a mental note of the information she had seen on the bottle and dropped it back into Vanessa's purse, placing it back on the corner of the table.

"See, no worries," Nadya said calming Serenity's fears.

She then took Serenity's hand and led her over to the dance floor, where her two young friends were doing the Twist with Aunt Cori. Serenity joined them.

Nadya tapped the woman to join her near the edge of the floor.

"Aunt Cori, it was truly a pleasure meeting you, but I think I'm going to leave before they get back."

"You don't have to do that. Vanessa has really shown herself today. I told you, I don't know what's going on with her these days. Sabien will get her under control."

Nadya had a good idea what was going on with Vanessa but kept quiet. "Please tell Sabien, to give me a call later if he has time."

Cori tried to convince her to stay, but to no avail.

Nadya grabbed her purse and keys and made her way out the restaurant to her car.

CHAPTER 17

"Why would you come here to ruin Serenity's birthday?" Sabien asked. "What's wrong with you, Vanessa?"

"I just came here to make sure my baby had a great birthday celebration." Vanessa straightened her clothes, and tapped her head, making sure every hair was still in place.

"Is that really why you came? From the looks of it you came to make sure she didn't have a good time at all. If you were concerned about her birthday, you would've had everything in order, as planned for last weekend, but since you didn't—I had to make something happen."

Vanessa dismissed his words with a slight wave of her hand. "It's a good thing I came in when I did, 'cause ya'll looked mighty cozy. Even got Tecora in on it."

Sabien cringed when his aunt's name rolled off Vanessa's tongue like the two women were the same age. He found it so disrespectful and she knew it. "Why do you care so much? You divorced me, remember?"

"Please know that Serenity Reese has only one mother, and no matter how many women you get into your bed—that's never gonna change," Vanessa stated with no hesitation. "Now if you don't mind, I'd like to go back to the party."

Without waiting for his response, she opened the office door, pushing it hard enough to bounce off the wall before she exited.

"With all that mouth she got, you would think she would know antihistamines can cause nosebleeds," Chloe uttered.

"Yeah, you'd think so, but…" Nadya responded.

"So you think she's bipolar or what?" Chloe questioned the presence of the pills in her purse.

"I don't know for sure. I mean, Lithium can be used for other things."

Chloe looked at her, "Chile' please. Are you the doctor or am I? You know good and well if it was prescribed for something else, it would not have said for the treatment of manic episodes on the bottle."

Chloe had a point.

Nadya didn't know how she would address what she found with Sabien, or if she should. Vanessa had a right to her privacy. But then again, Sabien may already know. After all, they were married for a few years.

It was now about 5:30 p.m., and due to Vanessa's intrusion, Nadya did not have the opportunity to eat anything at the party, so she was starving. She walked over to a cabinet in her kitchen and retrieved a fork from the silverware drawer. In the refrigerator was a container of hibachi chicken and shrimp that Chloe had picked up from their favorite Japanese spot. She pulled it out before pouring herself a glass of Moscato d' Asti.

Nadya joined Chloe on the couch, pulling her feet up into an Indian style position.

"You know I like Sabien a lot," she began. "A whole lot, but he has some baby mama drama going on. I don't know if I am willing to allow his issues with Vanessa into my space. Maybe this is too much."

"Wait a minute… hold up. This is the first person in quite some time that has brought that sparkle to your eye. I'm not gonna let you drop him that easily."

She gave her cousin a sidelong glance. "Whose life is this, anyway?"

"I really don't care whose life it is—all I know is that Sabien seems to be a pretty nice guy. Besides, he doesn't seem like the kind of guy who will just let go of a good thing when he sees it."

Maybe Chloe was right, Nadya considered. "We'll see what happens. And though I never thought I would hear myself say this aloud, I can see something more than physical with Sabien which is kind of scary for me. Now don't get me wrong, the sight of the abs and arms in those signature muscle shirts he wears—send fireworks through me. But I'm not gonna pressure him or be that desperate chic. I'll let him do what he feels is best. As for me, I'll continue to vicariously through you and Justin."

"Humph. Don't even try it. I know you still got ole' Banks in your back pocket."

"Shh… Shh. Turn that up," Nadya tapped Chloe's leg and urged her to increase the volume on the television screen as a photo of a mother and son pop up on the screen, with a headline that read: ***Woman Thought to Have Poisoned Son in Munchausen's Case.***

"…Prosecutors edge more and more to an indictment of Lacey Spears, who is currently facing charges of depraved murder and manslaughter in the death of her son, 5-year-old Garnett-Paul Spears. Though the child's medical records speak to years of sickness in his short life —severe ear infections, high fevers, seizures, digestive problems, Authorities are leaning more and more towards a different explanation. They believe it may have been his mother who was ill, possibly suffering from Munchausen syndrome by proxy, a psychiatric illness in which a parent makes her child sick to get attention or sympathy."

"Some people are really sick in the head," Chloe uttered. "But don't you ignore me, Missy Pearl."

"What?" Nadya turned her attention away from the TV screen to her cousin. "Don't start that again. I told you, I haven't seen him socially since our conversation during the Benefit Ball. Banks and I know how to turn things on and off."

"Sure, that's what you think. I'm not so sure he feels the same way you do."

Ding-dong.

Chloe placed her food on the living room table and got up to answer the door, pulling her over-sized t-shirt down over the butt of her tights.

She opened the door and turned to Nadya, "Caught the hint, eh?"

Chloe sashayed back over to the couch to grab her empty bowl and wine glass and headed to the kitchen to discard them.

Nadya eyed Banks standing near the door, looking as delicious as ever. She maintained her composure, grabbed a light jacket from the coat rack in the foyer, along with her flip-flops and stepped outside, closing the door behind her.

"Wendell, what are you doing here? This is definitely a surprise," Nadya admitted. "Since when did you start making house calls?"

Sabien pulled the car into the driveway of the stucco house.

He paused, taking in the sight of the exterior of the house. This was the first major purchase he and Vanessa made, after the success of the restaurant and the catering business. He was proud of it, because he knew it was a product of his hard work and dedication. Looking at it now, all he could think about was the hurt and pain that lurked in the shadows and consumed them over time.

Sabien got out and walked around to the other side of the car to take Serenity out. She'd had a pretty eventful day. Even with the fiasco of a party at the restaurant, it still ended up being a great day and he was happy to know he could do that for her.

Vanessa left shortly after their heated conversation in his office, and surprisingly enough, Serenity wasn't upset, probably because of the drama that ensued when her mother was there. She was however, disappointed when Aunt Cori told her Nadya had to leave. Sabien had to admit, he was disappointed as well. He couldn't blame her if she didn't want to see her again. Who would really want to deal with that kind of drama on a regular basis?

Sabien lifted Serenity out of the car and carried her to the front door.

He rang the doorbell.

Vanessa appeared at the door in a pair of his old jogging pants and a t-shirt that hung off her shoulder on one side.

"Can I come in," he asked.

"Sure, it's your house, too."

"Humph." Sabien grunted and slipped past her and climbs the steps to Serenity's bedroom where he undressed Serenity and found a pair of pajamas in her chest of drawers.

He removed the barrette from her hair, causing a cascade of auburn ringlets to encase her face. He placed her in bed, and before reaching down to turn on the night light, he hit the play button on her CD player.

Sounds of Mozart's *Contralto* rang out through

the cool air of her bedroom.

Sabien kissed her and walked out, leaving the door slightly ajar behind him.

Vanessa was waiting for him, leaned up against the door in a skimpy, barely there piece of lingerie along with sexy black heels.

He couldn't believe she was actually trying to condemn him.

"I'll let myself out," he said.

She stepped in his path, blocking his escape.

"Can we talk please?"

"Sure, I'll be in the living room." Sabien glanced at her. "Maybe you should grab a robe or something."

"We can talk in here."

"You do know this is not going to happen," he said, entering the bedroom they once shared.

"Why not Sabien, we are two consenting adults," she teased and rubbed her index finger from the top of his collar over his midsection. But before she made it any lower, he grabbed both her hands in his and pushed them back towards her.

"You were just cursing me out a couple hours ago and now you want me in your bed?"

"In *our* bed. Sabien, I recognize the error of my ways and I apologize. I know I messed up, but I really want us to be together as a family," Vanessa pleaded with him.

Sabien contemplated her words for a long minute. "That used to be the one thing I wanted more than anything in this world, but you were the one who decided I wasn't good enough, and you didn't want the marriage anymore."

"We weren't in a good place Sabien."

Was this really the same person he had been in a heated debate with just hours ago? It couldn't be. Her demeanor had changed… she was so mellowed out.

"And what makes us so happy now? Arguing with each other in front of children and ruining our daughter's birthday party? Not being able to agree on the best course of action, as it relates to our child."

Vanessa grabbed the matching robe to the nightie she was wearing from the bench at the foot of the king-sized bed, and slipped it on. Then she walked towards him giving him one last glimpse before wrapping it around her body and tying the sash. If this had been a little over a year ago, he would have taken her right there on the floor and ravished her, but the feeling wasn't there anymore.

"We can figure it out, go to counseling do whatever needs to be done," she suggested.

"Been there, done that," he said. "The best thing we can do is work as a joint effort to take care of our daughter." He strode out of the room.

"I'll let myself out."

Once he'd made his way back to his car, he sat for a moment before starting the engine. He'd told Chris that he would be back to help with the dinner crowd. Now he was having second thoughts. He hit the number on the speed dial for his employee.

"Yeah, Boss mon" his island dialect strong on the other end.

"Hey Chris. I thought I was gonna make it back, but I got somewhere I need to be. Can you handle everything?"

"No worries mon. Take care of you and yours." Chris hangs up and Sabien backs out of the driveway just as he caught the silhouette of Vanessa's frame vanish from view in the bedroom window.

He planned to do just that.

Nadya walked outside and squatted down on the top step. "I guess it's good that you're here. We need to talk."

He sat down beside her. "You're not going to invite me in?"

His gaze sent chills down her spine, but she was determined to ignore the desire he ignited in the pit of her belly. "This is not a good time."

"What's going on? Are you seeing somebody?"

"I'm not sure how to answer that."

"We have always been able to talk about anything."

"I've met someone, but I'm not really sure it's going, but there's something special between us. It's not something I expected--it just happened."

"Does this have anything to do with the chef?"

Nadya gave a slight nod. "Banks, it has everything to do with him."

"Are you sure you want to do this?" Wendell asked.

After a brief pause, she nodded. "Yes."

He looked out into the yard, and Nadya knew it was because he had enjoyed their arrangement as much as she had. But now she might have the opportunity to be in a promising relationship and if he would have her, Sabien was who she wanted it with.

He kissed her, his lips lingered for a moment, bringing to a close the special relationship they shared. "You know where to reach me if you change your mind," Wendell said before walking down the long walkway into the darkness.

Nadya sat for a couple minutes, and then pressed down on her knees and got up, arching her back like a cat. Before she could turn to head back inside the house, a voice stopped her in her tracks.

"I hope I'm not interrupting anything," Sabien said, casting a look over his shoulder in the direction Wendell walked..

"Of course not, please come in," Nadya offered. How long had he been there and how much did he hear? She wondered.

Inside, he said, "Listen I just wanted to say thank you for coming to Serenity's party today, and also for enduring the craziness that is my ex-wife."

"It's ok, I understand."

"Vanessa's behavior was out of order today. She felt bad when she thought about it." Sabien shook his head in confusion. "I really don't know what made her carry on the way she did."

Nadya recalled the bottle of pills that had fallen out of Vanessa's purse. She was sure that didn't come up in their conversation. She wondered if he knew about the manic depression.

"At least Serenity had a great time today," Nadya said.

"She did and was wore out by the time I got her to her mom's."

"She should be--just watching her made me tired."

"The man that just left... what is he to you?"

"Wendell and I work together. We had a thing, but it's over now." Nadya pressed her lips to his, surprising them both.

Sabien reciprocated, pulling her closer to him.

The heat and desire between them was evident.

"Don't go," Nadya whispered. She turned her cheek to feel the stubble of his beard on her skin. She wanted him.

"If you insist," Sabien responded with a sexy grin. "Lead the way."

Without a verbal response, Nadya's body language said it all as she pressed the door to her bedroom open.

Sabien advanced in her direction, closing the door behind him.

Chapter 18

After a long exhausting day at the practice, Nadya was ready to call it a day. Things had been non stop that she didn't have a spare moment to return Sabien's phone call. She had received several messages from him throughout the day.

Nadya removed her lab coat and noticed three files on her desk that were not there previously. She walked around the mahogany desk and noted the name on the tabs: *Serenity R. Marshall.*

She took a seat behind her desk, and opened the first of three files. Nothing out of the ordinary stood out in the first folder. She then pulled out the second file, and skimmed through. The office visits for nosebleeds was almost an exact replica to the first file. She took a look at the last file.

Three different pediatricians documented visits due to persistent nosebleeds. Somewhere in the conversation, Vanessa noted that she had been giving Serenity antihistamines. She knew that antihistamines dry out nasal passages and causes nosebleeds. She was instructed to discontinue the use of the medication, as there were no associated allergies that required the use of them. The next note following this event in all cases was one that said, *Mother called to terminate child as a patient with the office.* After the initial incident at the first doctor's office, every time it occurred thereafter, was reinforcement for her not to do it again, but she proceeded to do so, and it's right here in the files.

Nadya sat back in her chair with her hands behind her head, in deep thought. She then sat up abruptly and powered up her computer. After logging into the PC, she reviewed Serenity's chart. As she read the notes from all the appointments she'd had—all the reasons seemed like regular run of the mill issues a young child would have. The only thing was that the symptoms were mild to non-existent by the time she arrived to the office.

As she pondered over this, Nadya recalled the news regarding the mother who had been accused of poisoning her son to death with salt. She tapped her fingers on the keyboard for a moment before typing in: MUNCHAUSEN'S SYNDROME BY

PROXY.

She read aloud, "A disorder in which caretakers purposely harm children and then bask in the attention and sympathy." She'd heard about the disorder during a seminar last year, and the more Nadya thought on it now--the more it sounded like this situation with Vanessa. She needed to research this topic more. However, if her suspicions were right, Nadya had to figure out how to tell Sabien. She had to make sure Serenity was safe.

CHAPTER 19

Nadya and Sabien spent the next several months getting to know each other even more. The attraction between them was intense. What started out as a patient-doctor relationship for Sabien's daughter, had blossomed into something so much more.

It was nothing for her to come home to the table set for a candle-lit dinner, followed by a nice bubble bath, including lavender oils and rose petals. Or to a bouquet of lilies when she arrived at work. Ever since she found out stargazers were also Vanessa's favorite, Sabien bought her lilies or orchids.

Nadya also enjoyed surprising him at the restaurant. The moments she treasured most were when the staff were gone. He would break out his chef's hat and cook up something spectacular just for her. Those were special times because Sabien had opened her up to so much more than just tilapia and broccoli or salmon and broccoli, which had been her staples for years.

Their relationship had developed to the level of romantic getaways to places like Savannah and more recently to Asheville, NC. He had even joined her for an impromptu reunion of sorts with Nadya's med school friends. She wasn't sure how things would go and whether Sabien would see them as obnoxious, but it was quite the contrary. She quickly found that he adapted very well to his surroundings. When they discovered he was a chef, Sabien became the grill master by default.

Nadya and Serenity's relationship was a close one. Serenity gave her the opportunity to do some of the things she would have done with her own daughter, such as baking sugar cookies--something Serenity loved to do.

Since she started seeing Sabien, Chloe often remarked, "You have that glow."

"Chloe, what are you talking about?" she once asked her cousin.

"Whenever you talk about Sabien or hear his name—you get this warm radiance around you. You're falling in love with him."

Aside from Chloe and Justin, she hadn't been

willing to share him with any of the rest of her family, especially her mother.

Nadine had it made up in her mind that Nadya and Curtis were meant to be. Her mother constantly brought him up every chance she could. As for Wendell, he treated her the same as always, even though they were no longer seeing one another.

Nadya was relieved that Vanessa had not been a problem for them. She seemed to have accepted their relationship. Although she did tell Sabien that she wasn't comfortable with Serenity seeing the doctor that he was dating. Nadya transferred Serenity's medical files to her colleague. Serenity still came to her office, but was seen by another physician, Dr. Andrews.

Serenity put up a fight at the beginning but the few times she's been there since the switch, Nadya made it a point to pop in and say hi, so Serenity would be assured that she hadn't been deserted.

Although Nadya would have loved spending every waking moment with Sabien, she didn't want to confuse Serenity, so she seldom spent the night whenever the little girl was at the house.

Nadya was happier than she'd been in a long time. While she was fine with living single—it was nice to have such a handsome and wonderful man in her life.

***

It was the eve of Independence Day.

Sabien and Nadya took advantage of having a couple days off and a kid-free evening without Serenity.

"Did you ever think a date auction would lead to this?" she asked as they were relaxing on the chaise lounge on the 2nd floor patio of her townhouse. She leaned against Sabien's chest, who was sprawled out behind her. Nadya lifted her head at an angle, and felt the scruffiness of his beard against her forehead.

"Hey you… are you going to sleep on me?"

"Hmm…" Sabien moaned.

She laughed. "That would be a yes." Nadya flipped over to tickle him.

He winced from the change in pressure and then worked to block her hands as he was extremely ticklish and she knew it.

"Okay, Okay. I'm awake," he said as he held up his hands to block her probing fingers from reaching his sides and underarms.

"You are vicious woman."

"You like it," Nadya boasted. There were no words that he could offer as a rebuttal, because what she said was true.

He relaxed his muscles and pulled her into him for a kiss, by the collar of her over-sized shirt that she had claimed as her own since the first day she spent the night with him.

When they came up for air, she rephrased her question, "So did you?"

"Did I what?" he questioned. She sat up on his lap to straddle him, with her arms crossed, and a smirk across her face.

"Aww… you look so cute when you pout," Sabien teased.

He pulled her back down to him.

She remained tightlipped, not trying to give in to his antics. He tipped her chin until her hazel eyes were level with his browns.

"That night you were standing on that staircase, all I could think of was making you mine, and never letting another man touch you the way I'm about to, right now." Sabien silenced her with a sweet, tender kiss that made her immediately forget her previous aggravation as she melted into him. He maintained his palm in the middle of her back, and his lips remained connected to hers.

He pressed upward with his hips, signaling her to stand.

Once up, Sabien lifted her into his arms and carried her to the bedroom.

CHAPTER 20

"I guess I better never underestimate the stamina of Dr. St. James," Sabien said, leaning against the porch banister of Nadya's townhouse. They had just finished a four mile run on the wooded trail near her house. He was still trying to catch his breath.

"I thought I showed you that last night."

"That piano room will never be the same…" Sabien replied with a sly grin.

Nadya popped a rose bud from the bush and tossed it in his direction.

Sabien tried to distract her with wet, sweaty kisses on the nape of her neck and her shoulders as she unlocked the door.

Inside, they showered together.

She and Sabien had plans to see a few friends

before taking Serenity to Turner Field for the annual Fourth of July fireworks display.

An hour later, her master chef was in the kitchen at it again.

"Sit. I got this."

Nadya did as she was told and took a seat at the bar in one of her swivel chairs. She placed her elbow on the bar, with her chin resting snugly in her hand, as she watched him maneuver around her kitchen, bare chested and in khaki cargo shorts. This was a view she could enjoy any day.

"Sorry it's not much to choose from in there," she said.

"You know I can make due with just about anything." Sabien reached into the oven, with an oven mit and retrieved a small pan. When he walked away from the stove for a split second, to grab something out of the refrigerator, Nadya stood up on the foot bar of her stool to see what was inside the pan, and noted almonds.

She dropped back down as he closed the refrigerator, carrying two martini glasses, layered with goodness, over to where she was sitting.

"You had two green apples, almond butter, chia seeds, cinnamon…" he paused, hopping back over to the opposite counter to grab a bottle of honey and the almonds he'd just pulled from the oven, "…honey, and almonds." He sprinkled the almonds on top and the finishing touch was some cinnamon and a fancy design of drizzled honey.

"Bon appétit," he said as he handed her a spoon.

She dug into the first layer and placed it in her mouth.

"Boy, you are too much… keep this up and I just might have to marry you," the words slipped through Nadya's lips before she could catch them, and she kept her head down thinking he might not acknowledge what she'd said if she didn't mention it. But it was too late.

He smiled, before leaning over to kiss away the yogurt at the corner of her mouth.

She heard the soft buzzing of his cell phone.

"Sabien Marshall speaking…"

Something was wrong. She could tell by his expression.

"Is my daughter ok? …Yes, I understand. I'm on my way," he said and hung up.

"Serenity couldn't wake Vanessa and called 9-1-1. The police just got there and said they found her passed out in the bedroom." Sabien said, a hint of fear in his voice.

"Should I come with?" Nadya asked, not wanting to overstep.

"You sure you want to get involved in this craziness that is my life?" He asked, grabbing his keys from the banister by the front door, and then struggled to put on his shoes.

"I think I got involved, the day you cooked me breakfast." Nadya gave him a smile.

Sabien nodded. "I'd like you to come with me."

She slid her feet into her red Toms, grabbed her purse and rushed out the door after Sabien.

He looked so scared, it nearly broke her heart to see him this way.

When they arrived at Vanessa's house, two police cars and an ambulance surrounded the corner lot. Several bystanders and neighbors lined the sidewalks near the home, while others stood in their own yards.

Sabien rushed up to the front door, and was met by a female officer.

"I'm Sabien Marshall," he said flashing his ID in the cop's direction. "Officer Wallace called me to come over and get my daughter, Serenity."

"And your female companion?" The officer interrogated.

"My girlfriend, Dr. Nadya St. James."

Nadya showed her ID to the officer as well.

As soon as they entered the house, Sabien spotted Serenity dressed in her pajamas, seated on a loveseat in the formal living room next to another officer.

She caught a glimpse of him and wailed, "Dad-dyy...Daddyy..."

He scooped her up into his arms, hugging her tightly to his body.

After several minutes, Sabien asked, "Serenity baby, can you tell daddy what happened?"

No answer.

The female office that was with Serenity stood up and said, "Mr. Marshall, I'm Officer Wallace."

He shook her hand, and Nadya's as well. "From what I have been able to gather from Serenity since I arrived is that she woke up and went into her mother's room to wake her as well. When she didn't respond to her voice, she tried shaking her and still no response. So that's when she picked up the phone and dialed 9-1-1. The operator remained on the line with her until we arrived, and told her what was happening so that she wouldn't be scared to open the door for us. You have a brave little girl on your hands. You should be proud."

"I am," Sabien said.

"We found Mrs. Marshall unconscious upstairs, and these pills were on the nightstand." Officer Wallace held out a plastic bag containing two pill bottles and a pamphlet on Bipolar Disorder.

Sabien glanced down at the bottles and the pamphlet. "I know she was recently prescribed Ambien for issues with sleeping, but I didn't know about the other medicine." He then looked between the officer and Nadya, for clarification on the other, while maintaining his grasp on his daughter, "What's with the lithium carbonate? Is she Bipolar?"

"Lithium carbonate is used for the treatment of manic episodes, often found in individuals with bipolar disorder," Nadya stated.

Sabien seemed completely floored with this whole ordeal.

The front door opened, and two Fulton County paramedics entered, pulling a stretcher, at the same time that Vanessa was being escorted down the stairs by two officers who gripped her arms to steady her. Dressed in a pair of pajamas. Her hair was unkempt. She didn't seem completely lucid to Nadya.

Sabien handed Serenity over to Nadya, who instinctively carried her into a different room before she could see them place her mother on the gurney.

"Mommy's sick."

"Yes, she is, but she's going to the hospital where they will make her better."

Serenity laid her head on Nadya's chest.

"Your mommy's going to be fine."

The little girl's body was trembling.

She looked up when Sabien entered the room.

Nadya mouthed, "She's scared."

He nodded. "Come here, princess. No need to be frightened. Mommy's gonna be fine."

"I wanna see her."

"You can't right now. They are taking her to the hospital to rest. We'll see her tomorrow, I promise."

Nadya could feel the heat of his gaze on her. She knew him well enough to know that Sabien was upset. She couldn't blame him.

Sabien had watched the paramedics as they positioned Vanessa on the gurney, and secured her arms at her sides. Her head was turned to the side facing him, her eyes looking but seemingly not focusing on anyone or her surroundings. How could this be the same woman he had fallen in love with over ten years ago?

How could he have not known that something wasn't quite right with her? Truth was that he had a feeling that she was having some problems, but nothing to this degree. Had Sabien known about her condition, he would've insisted on Serenity spending the majority of time with him.

"You ok?" Nadya asked.

"I should have asked more questions."

"You can't blame yourself, Sabien."

"This changes everything."

Nadya reached over and gave his hand a light squeeze. "Why don't we get Serenity to your place? I'm sure she's hungry. We can stay in tonight to watch a movie or something."

"Fireworks," the little girl murmured.

"You still want to go?" Sabien asked.

Serenity nodded.

He pasted on a smile. "I'm gonna pack up some clothes."

Sabien went upstairs and walked straight to his daughter's bedroom. He blinked back tears. Losing his son had been the worst pain he had ever endured. Just the contemplation of any harm coming to Serenity... he couldn't finish the thought.

Until Vanessa got better, he refused to allow her anywhere near his daughter. Sabien intended to file for physical custody of Serenity.

CHAPTER 21

The ride back to Sabien's house was a silent one.

Nadya coaxed Sabien into relinquishing the keys to his Range Rover, allowing her to drive them to their destination. He sat in the back with Serenity.

She glanced in the rearview mirror to check on them. He sat with his arm posted on the window sill, and gazed out of the window. Every now and then Sabien pressed his lips down over Serenity's hair to give her a kiss, as she leaned against the side of her car seat, sound asleep.

Vanessa had bipolar disorder and Sabien knew nothing of her condition. Nadya couldn't imagine how he must be feeling.

She pulled into Sabien's driveway, and turned

off the ignition.

Sabien met her gaze in the rearview mirror. "Come on. Let's get inside."

He laid a sleeping Serenity down in her bed, covering her with a lightweight throw while Nadya watched from the doorway.

They went downstairs.

Nadya sat on the couch in the living room, trying to figure exactly what she was going to say to Sabien.

He joined her.

After a moment of silence Nadya spoke, "I saw the Lithium in Vanessa's purse, but I just assumed she was depressed. This happens sometimes after the loss of a child."

"How do you know about Jeremiah?" he asked.

"Your aunt told me. I'm so sorry, Sabien."

"It was a hard time for us."

"It's evident from the pamphlet that this is not just depression." She paused a moment before adding, "While we're discussing this, I need to tell you that I think Serenity's illnesses may be a part of her episodes."

Sabien met her gaze. "I'm not sure what you mean."

"I'm checking on some things because I'm not really sure, but if I'm right—I'll let you know."

"What can you tell me now?" Sabien asked.

"Vanessa's brought Serenity into my office on several occasions for symptoms that appeared to be non-existent or because of something Vanessa had given her. This seems to go back as far as age two per her medical records."

Sabien shook his head in disbelief. "Are you trying to tell me that Vanessa is hurting my daughter? She wouldn't do that."

"Why do you think she's changed doctors so frequently?"

"She's very picky. Nadya, Vanessa loves our daughter—this much I know. This is too much…" he said before making his way upstairs to his room without another word.

She couldn't blame Sabien for feeling overwhelmed. It was a lot to take in. She could only imagine that he somehow felt responsible, only it wasn't his fault. If only she could make him understand this.

Nadya stayed a little while longer making sure there wasn't anything she could do around the house to help before going home. She felt father and daughter needed some time alone.

Two hours later, her phone sang a familiar tune, and she smiled. "Hi there."

"Hi yourself," he returned. "Why did you leave?"

"I thought it was best."

"I'm sorry."

"For what?" she asked.

"For being a jerk. You have been nothing but great throughout this ordeal and I walked out on you. It was rude and I apologize."

She broke into a smile. "Don't worry. I won't hold it against you this time. You can't get rid of me that easily."

"Nadya…"

"I'm here," she answered.

"Thank you."

"You're welcome," she mumbled in the phone and they hang up at the same time. As she settled down to watch a movie, Nadya heard a loud boom and popping in the distance, as the first components of the fireworks show was underway.

CHAPTER 22

"Thank you for meeting with me on such short notice." Nadya was seated across the table from Wendell in the hospital cafeteria. She had called an impromptu meeting with Wendell to discuss Serenity's case.

"I figure this must be pretty serious if you're reaching out to me," he said.

"What do you know about Munchausen by proxy syndrome?"

He gave her a sideways glance, but realized that she was serious. He scratched his salt and pepper goatee in deep thought. "A very rare disease and often difficult to diagnose." He paused and then continued, "In most cases the primary caregiver concocts illnesses or symptoms in a child to prove he or she is a good parent. Why, what is this about,

Nadya?"

She reached into her satchel and pulled out Serenity's medical records.

"Ok... I'm trying not to make assumptions, but I really think Sabien's daughter is a victim of Munchausen's at the hands of her mother."

"I'm listening," Wendell said prompting her to continue.

"The first time I came in contact with Serenity, was a follow-up visit due to what appeared to be your run of the mill stomach flu. But over the past few months her mother has kept her out of school a lot for sickness that was never really evident whenever she came into the office. The last time I saw her professionally, she brought Serenity in to see me for a severe headache. However, the child said she felt fine. The mother insisted there was something more going on with Serenity, but the biggest thing that stands out to me is the nosebleeds."

"Nosebleeds?" Wendell moved in closer with his hands clasped above the table.

"Yeah, She was having nosebleeds. I found out the mother was giving her antihistamines, but according to Sabien, his daughter doesn't have any allergies. The antihistamines would have ..."

"Dried out her nose, causing nosebleeds."

"My thoughts exactly," Nadya said, placing her

empty tea cup on the floor underneath the table, so that she had room to spread the medical records out over the table. "After she came in for the headaches, I got a really crazy vibe and started to do some research. Three other doctors documented Serenity's mother bringing her in for nosebleeds."

She met his gaze. "The reason I came to you is because I need to know how to proceed with the information I have. The mother was admitted into the hospital on Friday after overdosing on Lithium Carbonate. Serenity was home alone with her at the time." Nadya knew nothing really came as a surprise to Wendell, but he really looked puzzled about this situation.

"I don't know how you can prove your suspicions, Nadya," he stated. "You don't have much to go on."

"I'm just afraid something worse is going to happen to her."

"Dr. St. James, I see you've got men all over, don't you? I'm sure Sabien would be interested in seeing you cozied up with a fellow doctor. Or has he gotten tired of you already?"

Nadya's eyes moved up slowly to join Vanessa's gaze. Her eyes weren't dazed and rolling like what she'd witnessed the day before and her hair was no longer all over her head. But there was still something vacant about her eyes.

Nadya placed her purse on top of the files to keep Vanessa from seeing them. "How are you feeling?"

"I'm perfectly fine. The day I've spent trying to convince the doctors to release me has been nothing wasted time that I could've spent with my *family*. My medication was much too strong."

Ignoring her sarcasm, Nadya said, "Vanessa, this is a colleague of mine, Dr. Wendell Banks."

He gave Vanessa a slight nod in greeting.

"Humph...nice to meet you, too."

Vanessa turned her attention back to Nadya. "How's my baby."

"When I left her yesterday at Sabien's house, she was fine."

Vanessa eyed them both. "This thing you have with *my* husband won't last long. It's only a matter of time before he sees right through you and what you are really about." She walked over to the counter to grab a drink before heading out the same way she'd come in.

"See what I mean?"

"Nadya, I know you care about this guy and his family, but be careful. She seems like a major piece of work, and you don't want anything to occur that you can't come out of," Wendell advised.

She gave him a smile. She knew he was genuinely concerned. However, Sabien and Serenity mean everything to her. She couldn't just walk away from them. She loved them both.

CHAPTER 23

Nadya approached Sabien's front door. She balanced a Bagel Shop bag and drink tray in one hand, while ringing the doorbell with the other.

She stepped back and stood closer to the edge of the stoop waiting for him to open the door.

She caught a glimpse of the cutest little face peep through the blinds at the side of the door. Nadya heard her yell, "It's Dr. Nadya."

The door opened and she was greeted by an even more handsome face.

"Hello beautiful," Sabien's raspy sleep filled voice called to her as he rubbed his eyes, with a lazy grin.

"Hello yourself," she replied. Even in gym shorts and a t-shirt the man was beautiful, she thought as she drank him in from head to toe, with a short pause at his broad shoulders and massive pecs that stood at attention.

Serenity squeezed between her father's legs, determined not to be left out. She was dressed in a Princess Tiara nightgown and matching bedroom slippers. Her curly mane was pulled up into a messy ponytail on the left side of her head.

"Did you come to play with me?" She asked.

Feeling unsteady, Nadya raised the goodies in her hands towards Sabien, and he relieved her by taking them.

"Thanks," she murmured.

Serenity used this opportunity to jump into Nadya's arms, and she carried her into the breakfast nook.

"Please don't tell me I woke you. I know Serenity is an early riser, so I thought I'd bring over some breakfast after my morning run."

"No you didn't," he said, placing the items down on the table. "As you can see from my living room, this little girl has been up for a while." Sabien pointed to the plethora of toys Serenity had spread all over the floor.

Nadya laughed and also noticed the pillow and blanket in a heap on the couch.

"So I take it, this is where you ended up last night?"

He nodded.

"Dr. Nadya, what'd you bring us," Serenity asked, not holding back, as she climbed up into a chair at the table and leaned over to sniff inside the brown paper bag.

"Serenity, mind your manners," Sabien said in a mock stern voice.

"It's ok. Really," Nadya came to Serenity's defense. "Well let's see, I know your daddy is a Master Chef, so probably nothing I have will amount to much next to what he can offer." She glanced up at Sabien with a cheeky grin.

He chuckled.

"We have blueberry bagels with honey walnut cream cheese and fresh fruit. And I have red berry smoothies for you and daddy, and a Caramel Mocha for myself." Nadya pulled the tissue wrapped bagels from the bag along with three individual containers of cream cheese. She placed a bagel and a cream cheese container in front of Serenity, along with her pint-sized smoothie.

"Yum, my favorite. How did she know that, Daddy?" Serenity asked, already licking cream cheese from her fingers.

Sabien raised his hands in the air and shrugged his shoulders, "I don't know, baby. I guess she's just smart like that." He smiled and winked at Nadya.

"Daddy can I take my food over to my table in the living room so I can see the T.V.?"

"Yes, Reese Cup, but don't make a mess. You have enough going on in the living room as it is."

"Here, let me help you." Nadya grabbed Serenity's bagel and her smoothie, and followed her to the living room. She smiled as she got Serenity settled at a little table with matching chair.

Nadya returned to the breakfast nook and sat down across from Sabien.

"So how was your night?"

"I did a lot of thinking."

She reached over and placed her hands on top of his, and he reciprocated the gesture and enclosed her hands with his for a moment, then released them, and delicately rubbed the tops of her knuckles.

"I'm thankful to have you in my life. It's just so hard to fathom all this."

"Tell me what I can do for you right now."

"Just continue to be the breath of fresh air that I need right now," Sabien raised both of her hands to his lips and kissed her knuckles.

"Eeewwww... Daddy's kissing Dr. Nadya," Serenity uttered.

"Hush, little girl, you don't know what you're talking about," Sabien said with a grin.

Nadya took a sip of her now lukewarm coffee and looked in Serenity's direction, "So what do you want to do today?"

"I want to go to the park, but first can I show you my new doll?" she asked. "Aunt Cori gave it to me."

"Sure, how about you go ahead upstairs? I'm gonna help daddy get situated down here and I will meet you in your bedroom. How does that sound?"

"Yay. Last one up is a rotten egg..." the little girl skipped through the living room and headed upstairs.

"Ok. I'm on my way." Nadya stood to clear the table, and put the place settings back in their original positions.

Sabien rose to assist, but as she leaned over the table, he walked up behind Nadya and pulled her to him.

The napkins and empty wrappers cascaded back to the table, as she turned to face him.

No words were exchanged—no words were needed. Her arms slowly rounded his neck and their lips were but inches away from one another.

Just as the smoothness of his lips touched hers, the doorbell chimed.

Sabien groaned in disappointment.

He held her gaze with his for a moment and finally released his clasped hands from behind her back, to answer the door.

She winked at him. "I think I have a little princess waiting for me upstairs anyway."

He gave her a quick forehead kiss as she passed him, with promises to join her as soon as he got rid of whoever was at the door.

Nadya made her way up the first few steps, but was halted in her tracks at the sound of a familiar female voice.

"Good morning to you, too. Aren't you going to invite me in?"

Out of sight, Nadya stopped her ascension to the second level.

Sabien stepped aside to allow her to enter.

Nadya took a few steps downward as if she were going to join them, but decided against it.

Making it to the landing upstairs, she entered Serenity's room, and found her lying on her bed asleep, with her twin American Girl doll wrapped tightly in her arms, dressed in the same pajamas and slippers as she.

Nadya smiled. *I guess that's what waking up at six in the morning will do to you.*

She gently rubbed the delicate curls away from her forehead.

Before leaving the room, Nadya glimpsed the photo of Serenity and Sabien. She smiled at the happy faces staring back at her.

What have I gotten myself into? She wondered, yet she couldn't walk away from Sabien. He meant too much to her.

"I was on my way to church and wanted to come by and pick up my baby," Nadya heard Vanessa say as she made her way quietly down the stairs. She wanted to stay out of sight. She eased down in the shadows of the staircase on a step.

Sabien could see her from his vantage point.

Nadya put both her hands together and placed them against her left ear, with a slight lean of her head, indicating that Serenity was asleep.

She stole a peek at Vanessa.

Nadya had to do a double take at the woman standing behind an arm chair in the living room. Is this the same person she'd seen two days ago, with disheveled hair and eyes rolling to the back of her head, being carried out on a stretcher? Vanessa was dressed in a black pin-striped pantsuit, with a white blouse, and black pumps, her hair pulled back in a tight bun at the nape of her neck. She even had a bit of makeup on, enhancing her high-cheekbones and slit of a mouth. Nadya had to admit, she was absolutely stunning.

Sabien released a heavy laugh as he came to stand up against the wall, just a few inches from the railing on the stairs, "I think we already know she's not going anywhere with you."

"I beg your pardon?" Vanessa retorted.

"No need to beg. I am dead serious," Sabien

said.

Vanessa's mouth dropped open in surprise. "Contact her for..."

"You want to tell me why I had to be summoned to the house by the cops, while you were doped up on some medication with our daughter there?"

When she wasn't quick with a response, Sabien continued, "I've been asking you for months what's going on. And you've been giving me the same ole' song and dance, about no work-life balance, being tired, but not being able to sleep. You put our daughter at risk."

"I agree, that it was a crazy, scary event, but it will never happen again," Vanessa promised. "Trust me. It won't."

"*Trust you?* You want me to trust you? Vanessa, our five-year-old daughter called 9-1-1 frantic because her mother wouldn't wake up. Is that really a call that she should ever have to make?"

Vanessa's eyes fill with tears, and Nadya feels for her a little.

"Something is really going on with you, and it's more than insomnia." Sabien was on a tangent now, and just when it seemed he was finished, he pressed on, "Then there's your obsession with Serenity's health. I'm beginning to think that what the doctors have been saying is true."

"And just what have *they* been saying? I hope you're not talking about that tramp you've been traipsing around town with on your arm," Vanessa snapped back at him. "I know what this is about. That witch has your nose wide open and you're listening to her lies."

Nadya felt her face grow hot.

She left the staircase and joined them, saying, "Everything I've told Sabien is the truth, Vanessa."

Vanessa's face flushed with indignation.

"It's strange that whenever our daughter's with me, she's completely fine—not even a cough, Sabien uttered. "But when she's with you, there's always something going on with her. And let's not forget how many times you've kept her out of school due to *illness*," he said holding his fingers up to emphasize his statement.

Vanessa stepped closer to him. "You're gonna take the word of someone you just met a little over five months ago over someone you've known for well over ten years? The person who you professed to love in sickness and in health? The mother of your children." Her eyes sent piercing daggers in Nadya's direction.

"The person I fell in love with is long gone," he responded. "The person I fell in love with would never leave a young child to fend for herself. But then again maybe you would... maybe you did...

twice."

Just as soon as the words escaped his mouth, Nadya knew Sabien regretted it. His expression showed that he knew he'd gone too far. But it was too late.

Vanessa slapped him. "*How dare you.*" Tears welled up in her eyes. "I'm a good mother. I would never do anything to harm my babies. I knew you blamed me for Jeremiah's death. *I knew it.*"

Sabien met her gaze, red hot anger in his eyes. "I don't know who you are, and I'm not certain of what you'd do and not do--you haven't been the woman I married in a long time."

Vanessa recoiled a bit at his words.

For a split second Nadya felt sorry for her.

"I am going to petition the court for physical custody of our daughter. She's not safe with you."

"Don't do this, Sabien. I'm getting treatment."

"You need more than pills. Vanessa, you should see someone."

"I will do whatever I have to do—just don't take Serenity from me," She pleaded.

"She's better off with me."

"And what do you think the judge would have to say about your girlfriend putting these thoughts in your head? That's a bit of a conflict of interest, don't you think? Besides, before you go stalking up my tree, you might want to pay closer attention to Ms. Thang over there. From what I saw at the hospital yesterday, it seems like you might have a bit of competition in a dapper older doctor. She and Dr. Banks were mighty chummy over coffee and a Danish."

Vanessa sauntered over to the front door, opening it. "If you want to challenge me in a court of law, go for it. Have your attorney call mine. But trust me, one way or another, you won't win." And with that she was gone.

Sabien turned toward her with both hands lifted up behind his head, and his chest puffed out. He closed his eyes for a moment and inhaled a deep breath, and then released it. Nadya moved toward him in what seemed like slow motion. When she reached him, and went to place her hand over his heart, he winced.

"I thought there was nothing between the two of you any longer."

"There isn't. Vanessa is just trying to cause problems for us."

"I think it's best if you go." He didn't even look at her.

She knew he was hurting and his mind racing, but with Vanessa's recent track record, he couldn't possibly believe anything was going on with Wendell based off of what she said. She hated to think things were ending for them before they even got started.

"Sabien, I…" Nadya says, but it is interrupted.

"I have had all I can take today, and now I gotta deal with going another round with this woman in court. I probably shouldn't have pursued anything this soon after the divorce. Serenity needs to be my focus right now. I don't need any other distractions."

Tears clouded her vision, but she kept them at bay. Nadya walked past him to the bar to grab her keys, and then headed to the door. She hesitated to open it for a split second, before walking out and closing it behind her.

CHAPTER 24

Chloe's bachelorette party was held at an exclusive nightclub called TJ's. If it was left up to her, Nadya would have stayed at home in bed, vegging out on her favorite Talenti gelato. The last three weeks since her blowout with Sabien had been too much to bear.

Though Nadya thought she would never allow herself to fall in love again. She had grown accustomed to their early morning runs, and late night chats. She couldn't wrap her mind around what it would be like not to have him or Serenity in her life.

She would love to be home right now, but Chloe wasn't having it, so Nadya traded in her scrubs and Toms for the black leather cat suit and a pair of red bottoms, Chloe talked her into when they were out shopping. As soon as Nadya's feet hit the pavement, all eyes were on her. Though initially apprehensive about her outfit, she saw heads turn as guys whistled and complimented her.

Maybe stepping outside of my norm isn't so bad after all. And she could definitely use the distraction.

Sporting a black sequined, strapless dress and gold pumps, Chloe was all smiles. On her head was a sparkling crown, and a *Bride-to-Be* sash crossed diagonally over her body. They entered the club and were led to a private table near the dance floor, where they found a spread of appetizers and various bottles of top shelf liquor along with orange and cranberry juice, ginger ale, and fresh olives.

"Let's get this party started right," Stacy, another bridesmaid exclaimed. She held her hands up and began dancing from side to side. The cocktail waitress broke the seal on one of the liquor bottles, poured a small portion in shot glasses, and passed them around to each of the ladies.

Nadya wasn't much of a hard liquor kind of girl, but she accepted the drink.

Once everyone was served, Stacy spoke up again. "To my girl Chloe on her bachelorette night. May this night be one to remember, before you make memorable nights as Mrs. Justin Bryant."

"Yeah," all the ladies said in unison, as they

tapped their glasses together.

They took their shots to the head simultaneously.

Surprisingly, the alcohol was a lot smoother than Nadya expected, although it did burn a tad bit going down. Drake's *Started from the Bottom* filled the surround sound of the club, and three of the women got up, dancing their way out onto the packed dance floor.

Nadya sat next to Ashlyn, another one of Chloe's bridesmaids, who'd already helped herself to a few buffalo chicken bites and potato skins.

"Girl, you want any of this to soak up the alcohol?" Ashlyn asked.

"Umm. Yeah. Let me get a few."

Ashlyn placed a few of the bite-sized snacks onto a plate and passed it to her. Nadya wasn't much of a partier, but she had an intense love for various types of music and loved people watching as well. TJ's was definitely the place to enjoy both.

She and Ashlyn chatted above the loudness of the club, laughing and joking over the sights and sounds around them. A young woman who appeared to be close to their age caught their attention. She was backing herself up in front of a man who could surely be her sugar daddy.

"Whew chile," Chloe uttered as she plopped down on the other side of Nadya. Bridesmaids,

Vertrice and Stacy sat down on another leather bench opposite them.

"My boo's got TJ's jumpin' tonight," Vertrice yelled as she sipped on her freshly poured Vodka and cranberry. Her boyfriend was the infamous DJ Spinz, and he was spinning records tonight in the DJ booth. The waitress came over with two ice buckets filled with ice and bottles of Moet stuck down in the center of each one. She placed them on the table in front of the ladies, then reached for champagne glasses on a shelf beneath the table, and proceeded to pour a glass for each of them.

Before anyone could ask where the bubbly surprise came from, she said, "These bottles are courtesy of the gentleman at the bar."

They all turned their gazes in the direction of the bar and Chloe immediately tapped Nadya on the arm. "Dr. Banks ..."

He raised his glass in their direction as if to say, "Cheers."

"Chloe, you been holdin' out on us girl. You know that fine specimen of a man?" Stacy inquired.

"Nah, that's one of Nadya's colleagues," Chloe replied.

"C'mon girl. Is that your boo?" Stacy continued to probe.

"Like Chloe said—he's nothing more than a co-worker."

Her cousin leaned over and asked, "Did you know he was going to be here tonight?"

"No, I didn't."

"From the way he's looking at you, he wants to rekindle whatever it was that the two of you had."

Nadya stole a peek at him, noting his lingering gaze. She downed her glass of Champagne in a couple of gulps.

"I'm gonna go thank him, and you should come with me." Nadya stood up and grabbed Chloe's hand to help her stand.

"Good evening, beautiful ladies," he said, putting down his glass when they walked over.

"Hi yourself," Nadya said.

His eyes soaked in the view of her body from head to toe. She immediately folded her arms over her chest, as if that would make her invisible. Nadya, clad in leather was something he could never get enough of, so who knew what thoughts were going through his mind right now. She absolutely could not allow herself to go there. They were done. Her heart belonged to someone else. Well it did.

"Thanks so much, Dr. Banks for the Champagne," Chloe said with a smile.

"It's my pleasure," he responded. Lifting his glass in a toast, "Here's to many years of wedded bliss to you and the lucky gentleman." Wendell took a sip of the brown liquid.

Nadya concluded that it was most likely his favorite… Cognac.

"Yes, he is a lucky man, isn't he?" Chloe chuckled before heading back to the rest of her crew.

"I'll be over there shortly," Nadya told her cousin.

She turned back to face Wendell.

He was still watching her.

Wendell rose from his barstool and took a few steps until he was standing directly behind her. The heat of his breath on the nape of her neck and the lingering scent of his cologne mixed with a hint of cognac, sent chills down her spine. He placed a hand on either side of her and held onto the bar as he leaned in until his lips were a kiss away from her left ear lobe. "I've missed you."

The heat at her core intensified and she felt her cheeks burning with embarrassment. Why did he have such an effect on her? Because she was in a vulnerable state.

She felt his body sway a little to the music and turned around to face him, pressing her palm against his chest, to push him back. "Wendell please don't. I told you…"

He pressed his index finger against her lips to stop her from speaking.

"Yes, I know you are in love with him. But

just because you can turn things off just like that, doesn't make me want to." He leaned in once more but this time as if he were going to kiss her, but she turned her head, to the right, and what she saw broke her heart.

Sabien was standing in the aisle leading back out to the dance floor with his hands hidden in the pockets of his dark denim jeans. Nadya's eyes moved up his body taking note of his V-neck black shirt and the grey blazer she bought him for his birthday. His eyes were ablaze and if looks could kill she would be dead where she stood.

With power she didn't have before, Nadya pushed Wendell several steps back, trying to make her way to Sabien, but he had already turned to walk away, heading for the club's exit.

"Sabien *wait*," she shouted, her adrenaline pumping even more in her veins, as she ran after him.

Just as she neared the VIP section, Chloe was coming towards her, "Nadya, the chef is in the building," she warned. She turned her gaze in the direction Nadya was headed, and saw the back of Sabien's head.

"Chloe, I need to go…" Nadya pushed past her, following Sabien's path out the door. Rushing out the door, she wanted to catch him and explain.

Panting out of breath, she yelled to him, "Sabien, please. *Wait.*" Though she was in shape, she didn't make a habit of running in high-heeled shoes, especially ones that haven't been broken in.

He paused in his tracks to allow her to catch up with him.

"It's not what you think," she said.

His back was to her.

She touched the elbow of his jacket. Sabien jerked around to face her, and what she saw in his eyes was worse than what she had seen at the bar... hurt.

"What is it that you could possibly say right now," he questioned, as he clasped his hands together behind his head.

"I didn't know he was going to be here. I swear. He had a bottle of Moet sent over to our table to congratulate Chloe."

"And let me guess," Sabien uttered. "That was your way of thanking him? Letting him grope you?"

"You don't want me, so why does it really matter?"

"I took some time over the past few weeks to think about everything that happened and I was willing to give you the benefit of the doubt. I really felt like we had something that was going somewhere. Even though Vanessa saw you with him, I thought, *hey, who am I to judge.* I can't be so critical with an ex-wife on the verge of a nervous breakdown."

Nadya folded her arms over her chest to hold in the warmth her body heat offered in the chill of the night.

"I remembered you mentioning you were coming here for Chloe's bachelorette, so I thought I would surprise you."

"Sabien, trust me when I say there is nothing there. It hasn't been since before our first date."

She heard footsteps behind her and turned to see both Wendell and Chloe walking toward them. Nadya rolled her eyes upward. This was the last thing she needed—Wendell and Sabien having any type of conversation.

"She's all yours, doc," Sabien said as he turned, and walked briskly across the street.

Nadya was left stone still, with the tears she tried to keep at bay, slowly streaming down her face.

Chloe wrapped her arm around her, comforting her in a tight embrace. Nadya leaned her head on her cousin's shoulder and cried. She stared at the dusty trail Sabien's car left in its wake.

CHAPTER 25

Nadine St. James had really outdone herself this time. As Nadya walked back and forth between the kitchen and the sun porch, she couldn't help but smile. Her mother was very excited about the dinner party she was hosting for Chloe and Justin.

She offered to throw the event after her sister-in-law and nieces had done such a tacky job with Chloe's bridal shower. Appetizers and finger foods for Nadine did not consist of wing dings and macaroni and cheese. Nor did shower gifts mean G-string lingerie and sex toys. Nadya recalled the look on her mom's face when Vertrice volunteered to demonstrate how to use one of the toys. The memory prompted laughter from her.

She laughed so hard she was crying. Nadya

had to place the sautéed asparagus on the wicker credenza to keep from dropping the warm dish.

"What was that, sweetheart?" Nadine asked from the kitchen.

"Uh… nothing Mom." Nadya cleared her throat and dabbed at her eyes.

"What are you out here chuckling about? We haven't seen those dimples come to life in weeks," Nadine commented as she stepped onto the veranda and ran her hand across the linen-clad table to smooth out a ripple in the material.

Nadya's smile slowly faded as quick glimpses of *that night* flickered through her mind. Images of those hollow brown eyes pierced her soul. She used her hands to quickly fan her eyes, biting back the tears, and glanced at her face in one of the stainless steel covers of the chafing dishes.

"Nadya dear, are you ok?" Her mother questioned with concern.

"Whew, I think it's time for me to switch out my contacts for the next set," Nadya explained.

"I tell you all the time to put that kind of stuff on your calendar," her mother stated.

"It's crazy to me that you can keep every appointment and meeting between the practice and the hospital, but can't keep up with changing your contacts. What am I going to do with you?"

Nadya formed her hands into puppets off to

her sides, and mimicked her mother.

She heard the chime of the doorbell and soon after the house was filled with the booming voice of her uncle Nathan, followed by his wife Audrey, and the happy couple.

Saved by the bell.

"Uncle Nate," she called to her dad's brother.

"Dia baby," he said with his arms outstretched. He planted a kiss on her cheek.

She whispered in his ear, "Thanks for saving me."

"You know I got you," he whispered back before releasing her.

"Aunt Audrey, I know that's my favorite red velvet cake in there."

Her aunt smiled and hugged her around her shoulders.

Chloe came over and bounced her hip off of her cousin's playfully. "And why have I never seen this dress?" she asked, regarding the fashionable, chiffon maxi dress Nadya was wearing.

"Because some things I like to keep to myself, rather than sharing with my wonderful cousin." Nadya bumped her cousin's arm with her elbow, and took a step back to hug Justin, just as her mom walked in to move everyone to the porch area.

Everyone followed her lead and rounded the table to be seated. "Wonderful weather for eating outside Nadine, and everything is so beautifully done," Audrey said as she doted over Nadine's elegant place settings and décor.

Everyone else nodded in agreement.

"Oh, it's nothing. I was happy to do it."

"Aww thank you, Aunt Naddi," Chloe beamed. "Hey, who's the extra place setting for?" Chloe gestured in the direction of the open place setting.

This was the first time Nadya had paid the table any attention. She turned her attention to her mother, "Mom?"

Nadine clasped her hands together to her mouth smiling, "Oh, we might have one other guest to join us. Nadya dear, don't worry. It's not anyone you don't know. I just figured it would be nice for you to have a plus one for the evening. I would have suggested that you invite Sabien, but every time I mention his name, you change the subject."

Nadya's insides heated up with anger and embarrassment.

Sensing her frustration, her mother said, "Now, now Dear, there is no use getting upset for nothing. It's not definite if the guest will even show."

The family began eating and as if on cue, Dominic walked in through the garage. "Hey, looks like I got here just in time," he said from the doorway of the patio. "Oh, and look who I found on the stoop, Naddi. He looked kind of hungry, so I told him we could spare some table scraps."

Nadya eyed Curtis.

"Stop it, Dom," Nadine said as she rose from her seat to welcome Curtis with a hug. "So glad you could join us, Curtis."

Nadya was speechless, and could feel the color draining from her face.

Chloe squeezed her knee under the table.

"Thanks for having me, Mrs. St. James," he replied, handing her a bottle of wine.

"Thank you, dear." Nadine glanced at her daughter. "Curtis brought your favorite, Nadya." She smiled and lifted the bottle for all to see.

Of course he did. She couldn't believe her mother would do this to her. But then again, her parents had no idea of the real reason they had broken up. An aching feeling tore at her heart as she thought about the realness of this situation. Curtis was everything her parents wanted in a husband for their only child. He graduated top of his class, and had received various accolades in his field since becoming a surgeon. He came from a good family, and in almost all accounts was an all-around good guy. She just couldn't get over the past.

"Nadya?" the sound of her name propelled her back to reality. Curtis was standing behind the chair next to hers and all eyes were on her.

"Dear, give him some room," her mother said.

Nadya slid her chair slightly to the left, noticeably annoyed. She had pretty much lost her appetite as soon as she laid eyes on Curtis.

She ignored him throughout most of the meal, although he tried to make small talk. Nadya pushed her chicken back and forth with her fork. She sent a glare in her mother's direction.

Nadine pretended not to notice.

"I have to say that I'm looking forward to being a grandmother," her aunt said.

"Mama, can Justin and I make it down the aisle before you start planning our family?"

Everyone laughed except Nadya—even Curtis which infuriated her. She turned to him as he scooped a forkful of lemon pie into his mouth, "So it's just that easy for you, huh?"

Chloe reached for her arm, which was now extended next to her plate, her hand clutched into a fist.

She pulled away from her cousin. She would not be silent any longer. "Of all places to boost your career, you had to come here. Why? And you had the audacity to come to my parent's house— to sit here, eat and mingle with *my* family. You... don't... have... that... right." she emphasized each word.

"Nadya St. James, you will stop this right

now," Nadine said.

"With all due respect, Mrs. St. James…" Curtis laid his fork across the small dessert plate, and wiped his mouth with the cloth napkin that previously covered his lap.

"Oh no. Don't dismiss yourself now. But then again that seems to be what you are good at… walking out. Since you have gotten so chummy with my parents, why don't you go ahead and tell them why you dropped their daughter off at home after a visit to an abortion clinic, and never looked back?"

In any normal circumstance, Nadya wouldn't have made this big a scene, but she had held this in for almost six years. Chloe was the only person who knew the agony she had endured. She bit back the tears that threatened her eyes, because she refused to allow him the satisfaction of seeing this type of emotion from her. Nadya glanced around the table, and it was as if things were happening in slow motion.

Her father squeezed her mom's wrist and she slowly dropped back to her seat, her eyes never leaving Nadya.

All the emotions she had held onto since that day came rushing back, but was in the form of anger. The day of the abortion flashed before her eyes as if it just happened.

"Mom, I'm sorry you have to look at me with such disappointment." Nadya started to tremble as the reality of this situation hit her.

She turned to her cousin, saying, "Chloe, I'm so sorry for ruining your night, I didn't want to make this about me."

Nadya took one final look in her parents direction, noting the glint of something in her mother's eyes, but not quite sure what to make of it. Her father leaned over his plate, hands clasped under his chin, with his eyes set on Curtis.

"Sorry I can't stay for dessert... Curtis can have my share." And with that, Nadya lifted one side of her dessert plate at an angle, and flipped it over onto Curtis's lap. She pushed her chair back, tossed her linen napkin on her plate, and headed for the door. She couldn't breathe. She had to get out of there.

CHAPTER 26

It was half past nine when Nadya reached her townhouse. Wiped out by overflowing emotions, she walked in, closed the door behind her, and kicked off her shoes in the mudroom, before heading to the one place in her house that could grant her the most comfort.

The thick darkness enveloped her as she walked effortlessly across the floor toward the piano.

She pulled the beaded string on the lamp and the room exploded in light.

Nadya sat down on the piano bench and delicately placed her hands along the ebony and ivory keys. She took a deep breath and slowly brought the instrument to life.

For a while, Nadya allowed herself to get lost in the low and high tones of the melodious sound.

Fresh tears flowed down her tear-stained face. The music intensified and then digressed into a melancholy tone.

The music slowly faded and she pounded the top of the piano with her fists, reflecting on the shambles her personal life had become. The chance at happiness that she finally thought she would have with Sabien was now null and void. And how could she blame him? He already had enough craziness going on with his ex-wife—he didn't need Nadya's baggage to muddy the waters any further. She couldn't believe her love life had been revived to be turned upside down all over again.

Visions of an adorable little girl invaded her brain. She had stolen Nadya's heart even before she had spent any time with her father. Though Sabien denied that Vanessa could be so heartless and vindictive to hurt her own child, Nadya knew in her heart of hearts that something wasn't right. But Serenity was no longer her patient.

Nadya finally rose from the bench to head into her room. Just as she pulled the beaded string once more, cloaking the room in darkness again, her doorbell rang.

She peeked through the faux wood blinds on the side window pane. Taking a deep breath, she rubbed the backs of her hands across her cheeks, and opened the door.

"Daddyyy," she wailed as he walked in, placed a bag on the banister, and enveloped her in his arms.

"Now it all makes sense to me," her father said. "When I initially contacted Curtis about the opening, he was stunned that I would be reaching out to him. When I asked him why, he just said he was relieved there were no hard feelings after the way the relationship ended. He said he felt you guys made the best decision for yourselves at the time."

Nadya sat up from her crouched position under the covering of her father's arm and looked at him with tears in her eyes.

"Dia…all this time, your mother and I were under the impression that your breakup was just that. I never really thought you needed to be in a relationship in med school anyway because of the rigorous coursework."

He patted the spot next to him, gesturing for her to come closer, and she obliged, nestling back down in the safety of her father's side as he wrapped his arm back around her.

Nadya couldn't be upset with her father for contacting Curtis about a job opening because she knew that Curtis was quite proficient at his craft, and her father had kept up with his progress over the years, and knew he was a stellar young surgeon. Of course he would reach out to him. And though she wanted to continue to hate Curtis, she was facing the reality of the decision they made together. No matter how much it hurt to think she had let go of that small part of herself to hold on to someone that did not really want to be kept, she had to take ownership of the decision they made. But the hurt of his disappearance, after the abortion, was what really made the decision so hard to bear, because she had to deal with the pain of it alone. Of course she had Chloe, but it should have been him.

She and her dad sat in silence for what seemed like hours before he finally said, "Baby girl, don't hold this against your mother. She really means well."

"I know Daddy but I feel like I'm suffocating at times," she paused behind a few sniffles, and then continued, "I mean who does she really think wants to be alone and unhappy? I sure don't, but the load of this situation has been so hard to bear…" her voice trailed off as she thought of her coping mechanism for being emotionally detached from anyone of the opposite sex. There was no way she could tell her dad about her involvement with Wendell. They were colleagues and she knew that he would be beyond mad. She had already seen enough disappointment in her parents' eyes. She couldn't add more.

Dominic took her chin between his forefinger and thumb, and turned her head to face him.

"You will never know how very proud I am of you. I think about you enduring so much alone, and in the midst of med school and your residency, and how you finished at the top of your class, and have done tremendously well for yourself since moving back home and starting your career as a pediatrician. I hate that you felt you had to keep something like that from your mom and I, but I could never be disappointed."

Nadya's chin trembled as she succumbed to the water works again. Dominic pushed the tears away with the pad of his thumb and kissed his daughter on the cheek. As he pulled back, her stomach growled.

"Ah... I almost forgot. Your mother packed you some food," he noted, rising from the couch and heading back over to the counter where he had dumped the brown paper bag when he arrived. He pulled out a covered dish packed with roasted chicken, sautéed spinach, and rice pilaf.

Nadya smiled through her tears as she accepted the plate from her father, noting how her mother had ensured everything was in its own section, and nothing was touching... just how she liked it.

"She knows you well, huh?" Dominic said, as if reading her mind. That she did, Nadya thought to herself.

"So since we are having a moment, care to share what happened with you and Sabien?"

Nadya poked at the roasted lemon, garlic chicken, not raising her eyes to look at him.

"I may be an old man, but I know how it looks and feels to be in love, and you've got it. He brought out something in you that I have never seen."

"Things are all messed up, Daddy. He doesn't want to be with me."

"Baby girl, money truly isn't everything, but anyone that will spend ten thousand on a date with a stranger has to know a good thing when they see it. And I'm not just saying this because you are my daughter." He winked. "Now eat up…we've got us some red velvet cake that we need to delve into."

CHAPTER 27

"Serenity baby, Daddy's gotta go." Sabien pleaded with his five-year-old daughter who had wrapped herself up into a human pretzel around his torso, as a means to keep him from leaving her home with Aunt Cori that evening. He worried for a bit because she had been really clingy over the last couple weeks. Especially on days like today, when she was due to visit with her mother.

Since he was granted temporary physical custody, Serenity's visits with Vanessa were mostly on the weekend due to her work schedule. She had decided to increase her class load since their daughter was living with him. It was not something he wanted to do--he never wanted to keep Serenity from her mother and he knew Vanessa was hurt by his actions. However, he had to do what he felt was best for his daughter.

For the most Serenity had adjusted well to living with him, but he'd noticed some minor changes in her. Every time she returned home afterward, she was sassy and distant for a day or two. Sabien tried to remain neutral when it came to her mother, but he had expressed his concerns, on several occasions, to his aunt who assured him that there was nothing out of the ordinary. Children could be just as moody as adults, she'd told him.

"Listen," he said pulling Serenity back from him so he could stare into her eyes. Tomorrow, it will be me and you, and we can do whatever you want. But today, Daddy's gotta go to work and you get to go spend some time with Mommy."

She wrapped her arms tightly around his neck once again.

Sabien bent over so his upper body was parallel to the floor and Serenity's little legs dangled to the floor, but her arms remained tightly fastened around his neck.

"But I wanna go to work with you, Daddy. I can be your little helper. Please Daddy, please. I don't want to go to the park with Mommy. I want to go see Dr. Nadya."

It took everything for Sabien not to call one of his Sous chefs to take care of the wedding reception, or to give in and let her tag along. Noting the time, he gestured to Aunt Cori for some help.

Walking over to Sabien, she placed her palm on Serenity's back and rubbed in a circular motion, "Now, now baby doll. Daddy's gotta go, but the quicker you let him go, the quicker he will come back to you."

Serenity lifted her eyes in Aunt Cori's direction, while she rested her head on her daddy's shoulder, maintaining her current position in his arms.

"Besides who's gonna lick the bowl after I mix up the batter for this pound cake?"

The little girl's eyes brightened immediately.

"Me, me, me..." she proclaimed, raising her hand high in the air, loosening her grip on her Sabien's neck. She slid down his frame, "I'll get the mixing bowl and the big brown spoon," she said as she skipped to the kitchen.

"Thanks Auntie. Any other day, I would drop things and stay home, but I can't today." He looked at her and knew no more words were needed.

"Aw, gone wit' all dat, just make sure you make it right," she said shooing him off.

Sabien gave her a side eye, and dodged her hand as he wrapped his arms around her and kissed her cheek. He then turned to open her screen door.

"Don't give me that look. I know where your heart is, you just need to remember too, and know that no one is perfect and everyone has a past."

Sabien paused and turned back towards the matriarch of his heart. "Love you, too."

"Bye munchkin. I'll see you tonight and get ready to stay up late with a little Princess Tiana and our favorite snacks," he called to Serenity in the other room.

"Bye Daddy," Serenity appeared in the doorway wearing the oversized apron Aunt Cori had deemed as hers.

Sabien smiled as he walked out and closed the door behind him.

He pulled up to the *Chateau Le Mon* at about 11:45am, with his team. All the food had been prepped over the days prior, and a few items his team had cooked at the restaurant, with the final touches to be made here onsite.

Sabien turned off the ignition, released his seatbelt, and leaned forward, pressing his head to the steering wheel in front of him. He was still slightly bothered over his encounter with Serenity at Aunt Cori's. He contemplated going back several times on the drive over, but stayed the course, and now thinking about it, he didn't even remember driving here. His mind was in so many different places from Serenity to Vanessa to Nadya.

He had to admit he missed her.

A tap on the passenger side window brought

him out of his trance. He looked in that direction and saw Chris. He rolled the window down.

"You good, boss?"

"Yeah man, just putting everything into perspective for today. Did we get the crab cakes from the fridge?"

"Yeah it's all 'dere. No worries," he responded with his island drawl.

"Aight, I'm on the way in."

"Bet," Chris tapped the side of the car before he turned and walked towards the catering truck.

Sabien rolled the window up, leaned his head back against the headrest, and took a deep breath. He tapped his hands on the steering wheel as if to give himself a jumpstart.

"Let's get this show on the road, Chef," he muttered to himself, reaching to the backseat of the Range Rover to retrieve his flavor pouch.

Sabien opened the door, and stepped out to the most beautiful sight, even though she was dressed in tights and a salmon pink t-shirt, her beauty still shined through.

He watched as she grabbed two large garment bags and a black case out of a vehicle. A warm sensation coursed through his veins—it was the same feeling he felt when holding her in his arms.

He started to call out to her, but momentary pride held him back. Sabien hoped she would look his way, but she didn't—she kept her gaze straight ahead. Sabien was no longer angry with Nadya over the events that transpired the last time they were together. The conversation he'd had with Chloe during their final catering meeting for the reception, probably helped with his recent resolve. But even after that, pure stubbornness kept him from reaching out to her. Seeing Nadya now—Sabien knew it was time to mend some fences. He just hoped it wasn't too late.

Chapter 28

Nadya entered the bridal suite just as she was about to lose her grip on the garment bags and accessories in her hands.

"Welcome to Mrs. Bryant's suite," Stacy said.

"Hey girl," Nadya said.

Nadya hung up the garment bags on a nearby clothes rack. As she moved deeper into the suite, her nose caught the succulent aromas of what had to be the most decadent culinary delights. She ventured into the suite's kitchenette where she found an assortment of brunch dishes, consisting of tart-sized quiches, smoked salmon toast, apple compote parfait, almond cinnamon buns, fruit cups, and peach melba mimosas. Her eyes lingered over the parfait and mimosas.

She smiled at a memory of Sabien creating

this breakfast treat after their first run together.

"Have you seen him yet?" Chloe asked from behind her.

"As a matter of fact I have," Nadya replied. "I saw him briefly in the parking lot."

"Are you ready to talk to him yet? He seemed quite remorseful during our chat the other day," she said as she reached over and grabbed a miniature spinach and cheese quiche from the platter.

"Chloe, you didn't…"

"How about, thank you Chloe." She wiped away the remnants of crust under her freshly manicured hands.

Nadya rolled her eyes. She really didn't want things to be awkward today.

"I just don't want him to feel pressured into anything. He was really mad that night at TJ's."

"Dia, you say that but it's me you're talking to, and I know how much you love that man. He loves you, too. Fate brought you together, and fate will keep you together. Once you get over yourselves."

"Twisted fate," Nadya murmured. "And what do you mean, get over ourselves?"

"You have to get to a place where you believe that true love exists, and you deserve to be loved. The past can no longer keep you shackled, whether it be decisions you agreed to or not," Chloe stated.

Nadya let her cousin's words sink in, then said,

"Enough about me. Today is about you. Let's get you married."

"Oh girls...you are absolutely *stunning*." Aunt Audrey gawked at Chloe and the girls as they stood in a synchronized pose waiting for the flash to go off for yet another shot by the photographer. She arrived about forty-five minutes prior, to capture all the before wedding moments, from the placement of Chloe's tiara once her fierce hairstyle was laid by their stylist, Chenora, to the penny being placed in her shoe for good luck by her flower girl, Alexis, Vertrice's daughter.

Once all the photos were done all the ladies took a seat so as not to break a sweat and ruin their beautifully made up faces.

"Oh, I forgot one last thing," Nadya said suddenly, realizing she has had forgotten to give Chloe her gift from Justin. She rushed off to the bedroom and returned with a slender rectangular box adorned in teal wrapping paper and a white bow. She handed it to her cousin.

Chloe ripped the wrapping paper like a little girl at Christmas. Inside was a tiny platinum star with a diamond cut in the center, connected to a platinum necklace. Nadya knew that one of their favorite pastimes was stargazing.

Rolled up next to it was a tiny scroll. Unrolling it and taking a moment to read, Chloe's eyes filled with tears but she was smiling.

"No, no, no ma'am. We need to get you down the aisle first," Stacy said, grabbing a few Kleenex's for her to dab at her eyes.

"He named a star after me. It's registered and everything," she showed everyone the copy of the certificate from the International Registry of Stars.

A twinge of something passed through Nadya. She dabbed at her left eye, just as a single tear approached the edge of her eyelid.

The wedding coordinator peeked inside the room. "It's showtime, ladies. Is our bride ready?"

"Absolutely," Nadya spoke up, walking over to Chloe to grab her hand so they could walk out together.

Chloe squeezed her hand as they followed the rest of the bridal party out.

"Twisted fate or not. Let yourself be loved."

CHAPTER 28

Nadya had yet to see Sabien during the reception, but she knew he was lingering in the shadows. She periodically felt the heat of his gaze on her. Leaning over the balcony, she took in the view of the crowd, and watched her cousin and Justin spin around as they danced the night away. They looked very happy.

"Is it wrong to say you look more beautiful than the bride?"

Nadya took a deep breath and turned around, coming face to face with Sabien. He was clad in his chef's gear including his flavor pouch and black skull cap, both of which were now draped over his shoulder. His eyes trailed from her head to her toes, as he drank her in. She immediately felt her core heat up.

"Probably depends who you ask." After a brief pause, she said, "Sabien, I..."

Before Nadya could complete her sentence, she felt the warmth of his spearmint-scented breath, as his index finger touched her lips to halt any further words from escaping her mouth. He lifted her head so that she had no choice but to meet his gaze again.

"When I ran into you that day in the parking deck, I never thought that anything would come of that encounter, even though the attraction was immediate. I told myself after the divorce, I was going to focus on me and Serenity. But you... you took my breath away," Sabien brushed a piece of stray hair from her face behind her ear. "Once I'd thought over things, when my mind was a little clearer, I knew I had screwed up and wanted to make it right, but then I saw you with Wendell."

"Sabien, it truly was not what you thought. When I took the job at Peachtree I was still holding on to some baggage from my ex-boyfriend. I was broken. Wendell was there for me--he was what I needed at the time."

Nadya reached for Sabien's hand and led him to the wooden bench near the railing of the balcony to sit down.

"Wendell and I have not been involved since before the Benefit Ball and when you and I took things to the next level, I didn't give him a second thought. It really caught me off guard to see him at TJ's that night. We have a working relationship and he has been an awesome mentor. He is well aware of what you mean to me and that I don't want to be with anyone else but you."

There was a pregnant pause between them for what felt like an eternity, before either of them said a word.

They were sitting right next to each other, but Nadya felt as though they were miles apart.

Sabien abruptly turned toward Nadya, straddling the bench with a leg on either side. He took her hand in his, "I want to be your present and if we can stand each other long enough, maybe even your future, too. If you will have me."

"If I will have you? There's absolutely no question about that. There is no chance on this earth that I'm letting you go again." She wrapped her arms gingerly around his neck and he stood pulling her to a standing position with him, leaning in for a passionate, tantalizing kiss.

It felt like an eternity since they'd been in each other's arms like this. Nadya savored the moment.

Sabien finally stepped across the bench, allowing his full body to come in contact with Nadya's. He wrapped his arms around her waist once again. "Um, keep that up if you want to become the main attraction rather than Chloe and Justin," he warned her.

Nadya laughed, allowing herself to be held securely in Sabien's arms. It has been quite some time since she'd had a genuine, happy gut busting laugh, and she needed it. "How's Serenity doing?"

Sabien smiled. "That little girl is still a handful, and thinks she's got me wrapped around her little finger. Just tonight she…" Sabien's voice trailed off as he felt his cell phone going off in his pocket.

He pulled it out and glanced down at the screen. Sabien answered immediately. "Aunt Cori…what is it? Calm down, I can't understand you. Serenity *what*?"

This was not the first time Nadya had seen this reaction from him, but her heart sank, as this time the color has flooded from his face. Something was terribly wrong. She leaned over trying to listen in and Sabien leaned lower so that she could hear Aunt Cori's voice on the other end.

Aunt Cori informed him that Serenity had broken out in hives and was having issues breathing, upon arriving back at the house from her visit with Vanessa.

Sabien was already in full stride walking across the floor to make his way downstairs. "What hospital? I'm on my way."

Nadya increased her pace to keep up with him.

They reached the bottom step just as Chris was walking by.

"Serenity's in trouble I gotta go. I'll call you later."

"Yeah, Mon.' I got dis, go take care of our little princess."

Sabien continued toward the exit doors, never once letting go of Nadya's hand.

Her parents met them at the door.

"Is everything alright?" Nadine questioned, her gaze trained on Sabien.

"Serenity is sick. The paramedics are taking her to the hospital. I'll call you later."

CHAPTER 29

The wheels of Sabien's blue Range Rover screeched to a halt as he pulled it into two parking spaces at the front entrance of the Peachtree Hospital ER. He snatched the keys from the ignition and rushed into the building, Nadya trailing closely behind.

Sabien and Nadia made it to the receptionist's desk, chests heaving up and down, out of breath. "I'm looking for my daughter... Um... Serenity Marshall. She... was brought in on an ambulance..." his voice trailed off at the sound of his aunt's voice.

"Sabien, baby..." Cori walked from behind a partition that separated the waiting area from the receptionist area, visibly shaken and emotional.

Sabien hurried to her, and grabbed her by her

elbows as a means to stabilize her, and simultaneously searched her eyes for some kind of sign as to what his daughter's current status was. Her eyes brimmed with tears as she tried to explain.

"Where is she, Auntie?"

"They have her in the back. They wouldn't let me go back there. Dear Lord… my baby."

Sabien placed his hand at the small of Aunt Cori's back, and led her to a nearby chair. He stepped to the side and allowed Nadya to take a seat across from them, while he chose to remain standing.

"Do you know what happened?"

"After we got home from visiting Vanessa, Serenity seemed very lethargic. I just assumed it was from the running and playing in the park. Shortly after we got home, I noticed her breathing sounding a little raspy and there was a bit of wheezing. I called the paramedics and then you."

Sabien ran his hand over his face and asked frantically, "So you went to the park?"

"Yes. I just had a feeling that I needed to be there. I can't explain it." Cori was shaking her head.

"What did she eat while she was there? Anything out of the ordinary?"

"They shared a turkey and cheese sub, some pretzels, and a juice box. Oh, and Vanessa brought some sugar cookies. She sent one in the shape of the letter S home in a Ziploc bag."

Sabien didn't find this out of the norm from anything Serenity normally ate, especially her mom's sugar cookies. "So where is she now? What are the doctors saying?"

Aunt Cori started to cry. "I rode here with Serenity. They gave her oxygen to assist with her breathing, then the poor baby went into convulsions, and was rushed in to see the doctors. That is all I know right now."

Sabien rocked back and forth with his head in his hands, trying to maintain his sanity, but at this point was doing a very poor job of it. He rushed back over to the receptionist's desk requesting more info, "Please can you get an update on my daughter? I need to know if she is ok."

"Mr. Marshall, I have sent word back that you are here and need to see the attending doctor. In the meantime, we really need to get this paperwork filled out so that we can get Serenity properly entered into our system." The pale, middle-aged woman, passed him a worn wooden clipboard, containing several forms with a pen attached under the metal stabilizer.

Sabien was frustrated, but conceded and walked back over to the waiting area. He sat down in the chair next to Nadya with a *thud,* and began to complete the paperwork.

Patient's name. *Serenity Marshall.*
Date of Birth. *April 17, 2009.*
Father's Name. *Sabien Marshall.*
Mother's Name...

Sabien hadn't even thought to call Vanessa until now. He took his cell phone from his pocket and dialed Vanessa's cell.

"Hi, you've reached the voicemail of Vanessa Marshall, please leave a message and I will address it when I am able. Thanks."

Beeeeeeep.

"Vanessa, give me a call. It's about Serenity."

Sabien tapped the red phone icon on his smartphone, and dialed the house. Still no answer. He shoved the phone back into his pocket. He was not surprised that she did not answer her phone, because she knew his number. But knowing that he would only be calling about Serenity—it wasn't like her not to answer when he called. He sat down and continued filling out the remaining paperwork.

Health issues for which patient is currently being treated for. *None.*

Allergies. *None known.*

Once completed, he dropped it off at the receptionist's desk, and blew out a deep exasperated breath, walking over to the panoramic window across from where everyone else was seated, with his hands behind his head, fingers intertwined. He felt nervous energy coursing through his veins, a sign that his patience was wearing thin.

Nadya walked up behind him and placed a gentle hand on his shoulder blade. "Let me go see what I can find out."

Sabien had no idea how the night would go when he approached Nadya at the reception, but he was glad that she was here with him. He was having a hard time remaining calm, when all he really wanted to do was run through those double doors and find his daughter himself. He finally nodded his head in agreement.

Just as Nadya rounded the corner of the partition to follow-up on Serenity's condition, she was met by Banks.

"Dr. St. James. You're dressed a bit formal for rounds this evening."

"Not on call this evening. Here supporting Sabien. Is Serenity Marshall your patient?"

"She is." They made their way over to Sabien and his aunt.

The sliding glass doors of the ER opened and in rushed Chloe, Justin, Nadine, and Dominic. Everyone stood in anticipation of what Wendell had to say.

Banks acknowledged Dominic with a nod, then turned to face Sabien. "It appears that Serenity has had a severe allergic reaction which led to anaphylactic shock. We are still running a few tests." He paused, this time with a look of concern etched on his face, and took a deep breath. "During the ride over, she did experience a few bouts of unconsciousness and had a tremendous loss of oxygen to her brain. She has been placed on a ventilator, and remains in critical condition. We are working to get her vitals stabilized before moving her to the PICU."

"Oh Father God, Lord in Heaven," Aunt Cori muttered full of angst, as her hands moved from Sabien's arm to cover her mouth.

Sabien immediately reached for her so she wouldn't collapse to the floor.

Nadya's father and Justin assisted Cori to a nearby chair.

Gulping back the sob that had lodged itself in his throat, Sabien asked, "Can we see her?"

Wendell nodded. "At this time we would like to limit the amount of people in and out of her room to immediate family only." He turned to head back towards the swinging doors leading to the interior of the ER, and instructed one of the attendants to accompany Sabien back to see his daughter.

Nadya knew from the tormented expression on his face that he was trying to hold it together.

She rushed to him.

She was encased in his arms, and he held on for dear life.

Nadya pulled back ever so gently, grabbed the sides of his face, and looked into his eyes, "Go be with your daughter, I will be right here." They shared a moment between the two of them, no words but eyes full of emotion.

He followed the nurse and Nadya turned to watch him head down the long hallway, with her hands clasped together under her chin, as she kept her tears at bay. Before they made it to the metal double doors, Sabien turned back to her and stretched out his hand for her to join him.

A lone tear rolled down her face as she rose.

When Nadya reached him, she took his hand as he uttered, "I need you with me."

CHAPTER 30

The walls of the corridor leading to Serenity's room were adorned with beautifully sketched images of multicultural children, in all facets of play and learning. A little girl was dressed in a doctor's uniform with the diaphragm of a stethoscope held up to a teddy bear. A little boy made his mark on the moon in an astronaut uniform.

Nadya noted how strange it felt to be on the other side of things, as they entered Serenity's room.

Sabien staggered in hesitation, as the wind escaped him for a split second at the sight of his baby in a hospital bed that was about to swallow her up. If it were not for the tubing securely attached to her face, to aid in breathing, and the *beep beep beep* of the cardiac monitor, she would look as though she was resting peacefully as she did in her sleigh bed at home.

The nurse checked the monitors and quickly exited the room, leaving Nadya and Sabien alone with Serenity.

Sabien remained frozen in place for a moment and Nadya moved a few steps forward, approaching the foot of Serenity's bed.

Where is her mother?

She knew Sabien had tried reaching Vanessa by phone, but to no avail. Something just wasn't right. She slipped out of the room and called the police department.

"This is Dr. Nadya St. James at Peachtree Children's Hospital. Can you please send someone to Vanessa Marshall's house? Her daughter is in the hospital and we've been trying to reach her. Her address is …"

When she returned, Nadya flipped through Serenity's chart, skimming through all the doctor lingo to see if she could offer any further information to Sabien.

He sat there brushing his daughter's disheveled curls away from her forehead. He then leaned down and kissed her. The kiss lingered for quite some time, causing a twinge in Nadya's heart, as she hurt for the man she loved.

Sabien pulled up a nearby chair and sat next to the bed. He nestled Serenity's tiny hand in his, and kissed it. "Baby girl…you gotta wake up. How are we going to have our date night… Daddy can't make it without you…" His voice trailed off as he tried to keep himself composed.

He stared at her as if willing her to open her eyes, but no response.

Sabien bowed his head and cried.

Tears stung Nadya's eyes as she returned the medical charts to their holder, and walked up behind him, placing her hands on his shoulders in comfort. He didn't look at her immediately, but when he did, her heart melted at the sight of his wounded eyes. She longed so much to take his pain away.

Nadya released her hold on him and walked over to grab some Kleenex above the sink. She returned to his side, handing them to him. She pulled up another chair, parking it next to his.

Sabien took a moment to gather himself and then leaned back in his chair, "How could this happen? Wouldn't we know if she was allergic to something by now, at this age?"

"Allergies can be detected at various ages, and often times it's not found until the person comes in contact with the food or substance unknowingly," Nadya explained. "We will have to wait for the tests to come back." She eyed Serenity. "I contacted the police to go to her house."

"I'm going to try her again." Sabien took a deep breath and released his daughter's hand. He got up and strode toward the door.

Nadya rose to her feet and leaned over to make Serenity as comfortable as possible. She lifted all the wires, tubing, and PICC line protruding from her body to ensure nothing was laying in an awkward position over her tiny frame. Glancing over at the cardiac monitor, there appeared to be no changes from what was already documented in her chart. Nadya gently rubbed Serenity's cheeks, noting how her beautiful pecan skin, appeared pale under the hospital lighting.

"Still no answer," Sabien uttered. "I even called the gym, and a few other places I figured she might be, but they haven't seen her. I don't get it."

Nadya secretly worried that Vanessa could be passed out at home, but kept her thoughts to herself.

Sabien reached over, to grab her hand.

There was a light tap on the door and the nurse peeked in. "Mr. Marshall, I'm so sorry but visiting hours are just about over."

Sabien caught a glimpse of his watch and noted the time. He stroked Serenity's hand a little longer, and when it seemed he would linger there for an eternity, Nadya lightly tapped him on his shoulder, signaling that they had to leave.

Sabien kissed his daughter once more on her cheek and whispered in her ear, "Daddy loves you. Always remember that." He paused near the doorway, taking one more glance in Serenity's direction.

Sabien and Nadya walked back to the waiting room. It warmed Nadya's heart to see her family, but hated that Chloe and Justin had chosen to spend their first night as man and wife here in the ER.

"You two should leave," she told them. "You're gonna be tired in the morning when you have to catch that flight to Turks and Caicos."

"Congratulations Mr. and Mrs. Bryant," Sabien said. "Thank you so very much for offering your support," his voice broke as if his body would follow suit at any time. He composed himself, then added, "Nadya's right. This is your wedding night."

Both Chloe and Justin stood up. Justin offered a handshake and Chloe, a hug and they left.

"Mr. Marshall..." Dominic offered salutations but was quickly interrupted by Sabien.

"Dr. St. James, please call me Sabien." his request was warm and sincere.

"Sabien. My wife and I are so sorry to hear of this mishap with your daughter. We are praying for a speedy, but full recovery. Please let us know if there is anything we can do."

"Thank you. That really means a lot," Sabien responded, then turned to Nadya, "I'm gonna go and check on Aunt Cori and let her know how Serenity is doing." He kissed her cheek and headed over in Aunt Cori's direction.

Nadya turned to face her family, "Thanks for coming."

"Girl, you know there was no way I was going to be able to go away without seeing you and making sure that little princess is ok," Chloe said. "The reception was pretty much over after you guys left anyway."

"Nadya, dear, is she allergic to any foods? Did she eat something out of the ordinary?"

Her mother's face was filled with concern.

"Sabien says she doesn't have any food allergies that he's aware of." Her eyes scanned the room in his direction, noting him sitting next to Aunt Cori, holding her hand, as they talked quietly together. Nadya didn't have to look in her mother's direction to know she is in disbelief. No one in her family, except Chloe, was aware of the craziness that had taken place with Vanessa and her mental instability. She glanced at her mom with a *not now* look, and Nadine backed off.

Her parents offered to stay, but with the results of the labs still out, it was going to be a waiting game. Nadya and Sabien found an empty corner in the waiting room to hang out until the results were back.

Chapter 31

Last night as the waiting area cleared out, she and Sabien were able to snag a few extra chairs and push them together for a makeshift bed of sorts. Of course there was not a lot of sleeping going on anyway, between worrying and not being able to find a comfortable position.

Sabien was up and ready to see Serenity as soon as visiting hours started back up for the day. Nadya decided to give him some time alone with Serenity. Her father had dropped off a change of clothes for her before his scheduled surgery.

Aunt Cori had kept in touch throughout the night. She had already called Nadya saying, "I'm going to be there around mid-morning. I didn't get any sleep last night worrying about both my babies. Is Vanessa there?"

"We haven't heard anything from her. I sent

the police over to her house but they said no one was home--her car wasn't there."

"Oh Lord… where is that woman? That child needs her mother."

Nadya agreed. "Oh, can you bring a change of clothes for Sabien. I know he's not going to leave the hospital."

After changing out of her wedding attire, Nadya checked in with the receptionist to confirm if anyone had followed-up with Sabien but they had not.

Nadya picked up a magazine from the rack and sat down, placing the duffle bag on the floor.

Wendell appeared before her.

"Double shift?" she asked.

"It has definitely turned into that," he gave her an exasperated look. Wendell placed his palm on his forehead, before running it back across his bald head.

Nadya sensed something was up.

He took a seat next to her. "I probably shouldn't be coming to you with this, due to the conflict of interest, but when these results came in, it made me think of our conversation back in July about Munchausen Syndrome by Proxy."

"And?"

Wendell pulled out Serenity's lab results and handed them to her.

Nadya perused through making note of the two medications listed. She was horrified.

What had Vanessa done?

Sabien sat beside Serenity's bed, his eyes fixated on her, willing her to wake up. He had hoped the Banks had figured out whatever this thing was that had a hold on his daughter. Sabien felt so empty without her. Her color wasn't the same bright and vibrant shade of brown, but had more of a morbid green tint to it. He still couldn't figure out why he had not heard from Vanessa yet, after leaving her several messages. When he called her earlier, the automated recording announced the voicemail was full.

Sabien leaned down and kissed Serenity once again on the forehead and tapped her nose with his finger which was their customary thing.

He walked down to the waiting area to give his aunt some time with Serenity. He greeted Nadya's parents before kissing her on the lips.

Just then Wendell returned to the waiting area. He pulled Sabien off to the side and gestured for Nadya to join them.

"Serenity's lab results are back and there are substantial traces of Lithium and Ambien in your daughter's system."

"That's the medicine her mother was taking. How did Serenity get them?" Sabien shifted his weight from one leg to the other and released his hand from Nadya's to cross his arms over his broad chest. He began trembling with anger.

"Where is the mother now," Wendell asked.

"I haven't been able to reach her."

Sabien turned to his aunt asking, "Did Vanessa take Serenity anywhere away from your view?"

"No, I was with them the entire time."

"Did they share any food?"

"Only the sugar cookie. Vanessa bought Serenity her own box lunch. She even paid for mine.

Nadya recalled the first time she made sugar cookies with Serenity and Sabien. Serenity had asked if they were going to put the powdered sugar on the cookies like her mother did. "We need to have the other sugar cookie tested," she blurted. "You said that she gave Serenity one to bring home."

"I think it's still in the car."

Sabien rushed out the doors.

Aunt Cori began to sob, grief stricken. Nadine rushed to her aid and led her to an empty chair nearby.

Sabien returned with the cookie.

"Why would she do this?" he asked Nadya,

who could only shake her head. "We're going to have to get the police involved. I'm so sorry."

He could only nod.

"Do you think Vanessa would harm herself?" Nadya inquired.

"I don't know anything anymore." Tears rolled down his cheek.

She hugged him. "It's going to be okay."

"Not if I lose my little girl. Nothing will ever be right again."

A police officer walked up to them. "Excuse me, are you Mr. Marshall?"

He nodded.

"I went by the house to see if your wife was there--"

"She's my ex-wife. I've been trying to reach her."

"Is there any place special she might go?"

"Other than home, she might be at the gym or the Culinary Arts Academy. She's on staff there."

"Mr. Marshall, we are going to do everything we can to find her."

As soon as the officer was nowhere in sight, Sabien stalked towards the door, but Wendell and Dominic rushed him before he could leave.

"Let me go. I need to find her. *Let me go*."

"No son, we can't let you do that," Dominic commanded. "Let the police do their job."

"She tried to kill my baby. She's the reason Serenity won't open her eyes."

They wrestled Sabien to the floor.

Nadya rushed to his aid, cradling him in her arms as he cried.

As bystanders looked on, their tears merge into a single stream, becoming one, as the reality of the last day's events set in.

What had Vanessa done?

CHAPTER 32

After the events of the morning, the day dragged on for what seemed like an eternity. Everyone was on edge. Serenity had since been moved to the PICU, so everyone was now seated in that lobby instead. She remained unconscious and was still on the ventilator.

Sabien was a nervous wreck, wringing his hands together and not able to remain seated for long periods of time. Nadya remained by his side every moment, although she tried to give him space when needed. She tried to reinforce that there was really no way he could have predicted this. Vanessa had never done anything before to Serenity that would make them think she would hurt her to such an extreme as this.

Though Dominic had several surgeries he had to scrub in for, he took time to check on Sabien.

Nadine was there almost as much as Nadya. She never requested to go in and see Serenity, she just wanted to be there in case they needed her. This unfamiliar side of her mother, warmed Nadya's heart. Not that her mother was unfeeling and uncaring, but not to be in the limelight and at the center of attention was new for her. In this particular instance, she appeared to be ok with someone else being the focus.

Cori spent her time reading the Bible and praying.

Wendell returned to confirm that the cookie was laced with Lithium Carbonate and Ambien. He also announced that they would have to get the police involved--it was now a criminal case.

Minutes later, Sabien received a call from the officer he'd spoken earlier.

Vanessa had been found stoic and unresponsive in her classroom. He was en route to the hospital with her.

When the call ended, Sabien crumbled to the floor.

Nadya worked to console him.

"There are no words. Truly no words. She is her mother. How do you do that somebody, especially your own flesh and blood? *Your own child.* Now I don't know if and when my little girl is going to wake up, but she still has her life." He looked at her, his eyes filled with pain.

Nadya tried to rub his back, but he pulled away.

"I just need some time alone," he said.

Although she wanted to be right there with him, Nadya glanced back at her mother, who gestured for her to let him go. So she did.

He disappeared down the hall.

Nadya walked to the front of the chapel, lit a candle, then sat down on the second row with her elbows resting on the pew in front of her and her hands folded in front of her in a praying stance. Nadya meditated until she felt someone sit down next to her.

She opened her eyes and it was her mother. Before she knew what hit her, Nadya was wrapped in Nadine's arms. She held onto her tightly as her mother rocked her gently.

Nadine leaned toward the edge of the pew to grab the tissue box and pulled a few to give to her daughter. They sat that way in silence for a while. All of a sudden, it was Nadine who needed Kleenex.

"Oh mom, please don't cry." Nadya comforted her as she dabbed at her eyes.

"I'm ok. I'm ok." She took a deep breath and finally spoke again, "You weren't my first baby."

Nadine's words baffled Nadya for a minute as she waited for her to continue. "What I mean to say is I was pregnant once, before I had you, even before your father and I were engaged to be married. Of course, you know during our college years we had a short spell where we weren't together. Somewhere in the midst of our hiatus, we had sex and I found out I was pregnant. I battled with whether or not to have an abortion because I knew a baby was the last thing we needed. I eventually decided to keep it. I'd planned to tell him that evening."

"It was raining so hard that I could barely see the street signs. As I rounded a corner, a truck coming in the opposite direction went over the center line and I didn't see him. My car ended up wrapped around a tree. When I woke up and saw him, he actually cried and said he thought that he had lost me, and vowed we would never be apart again."

Nadine fell silent and Nadya asked, "What happened with the baby?"

"They were not able to save the baby."

"Oh mom, I never knew that. I'm so sorry." She hugged her again tightly.

"Those were truly some of the darkest days of

my life, with recuperating from my injuries and dealing with the emotional strain of losing the baby, but your father—he was there for me."

Nadya could not believe her mother was sharing something so intimate with her.

Nadine turned to face her daughter and reached out for her hands, "I said all this to apologize to you. I remember what it was like for me going through my miscarriage, and I'm so sorry you didn't feel like you could come to us when you found out you were pregnant. You should have never had to endure any of that without the love and support of your family."

"I had Chloe," Nadya said through her tears.

"Yes I know. You guys have always been thick as thieves, but I mean without me and your father. It would have been hard to deal with, but we would have figured things out, and if you still chose to have an abortion we would have been there to support you in that as well," she said.

"When you blew up at the dinner party and told us what happened, I was just so dumbstruck because for one I couldn't believe what I was hearing, and then two, I was stuck in my own feelings thinking about the pain I felt during my own ordeal. It was like it was happening all over again."

You know I kicked that boy right out of my house as soon as you were gone, too." Nadya couldn't help but laugh. Her mom was so hard-nosed and matter of fact about things, she rarely let this side of herself come out. But she liked it. "To know he left my baby to go through that by herself, I wasn't having that. I might have really liked him, but I love you so much more." Though Nadya never doubted her parents' love for her, she'd always had a certain affinity for her father. She was daddy's little girl after all. Sharing this newfound bond with her mom was a nice feeling.

Nadya chimed in, "I wasn't mad at Curtis because we got the abortion—that was a decision we made together. I was angry and hurt because he didn't think enough of me to see it through and make sure I was actually ok. No one should ever have to go through something like that alone. For a while I thought I was right there at the cusp of crazy, and then one day, I had a long talk with myself after a swift kick in the pants by Chloe. Well, several kicks. I had to decide if I was going to allow myself to remain in a place of pity and mourning, or if I was going to achieve the goals I set for myself."

Nadya thought about Vanessa's mental state and wondered if they manifested after the death of her first child. She also wondered if she'd had the problems before the child died. She knew Sabien wondered the same.

"Mom, I'm really worried about Sabien, especially if Serenity doesn't make it. He's already lost one child."

"Hush now, we aren't going to entertain any such talk like that." She paused, "You love him don't you?"

Nadya nodded. "Have you told him?"

She shook her head no. "I never felt like the time was right."

"You know I would usually be the last person to tell you to put your emotions on the line for somebody, but that might be just what he needs now. He needs to know that you love him."

"You're right Mom."

"I may have released a little of my emotional side on you today, but I'm still Nadine St. James."

Nadya hugged her mom and they left the chapel in search of Sabien.

CHAPTER 33

Sabien and Nadya spent their days visiting with Serenity during visiting hours, and slept in the lobby at night, when visiting hours were over. The following Saturday, Chloe and Justin returned from their honeymoon and their first stop from the airport was the hospital. Chloe had checked in while they were away.

Sabien's crew at the restaurant, was a well-oiled machine without him. He checked in with them regularly, but his management team and Chris had things under control, which made his time spent at the hospital with Serenity more bearable, not having to worry if his business was being run in the ground. Nadya was able to rearrange her appointments for the week, or transfer her patients over to Dr. Andrews if an immediate appointment is needed.

Sabien had the chance to give Serenity a sponge bath, but he was nervous with all the wires and tubing.

After being assured by Nadya that she would do it with him, Sabien relaxed. She had been his rock from the very beginning of this ordeal, and even though he had his moment after hearing the news of Vanessa's capture where he didn't want to be bothered with anyone, Nadya let him have his space, but she wasn't too far away.

Nadya brushed Serenity's hair. She lifted her head in his direction, and Sabien saw her chin quiver. He beckoned her over to sit with him and she obliged.

"What is it, baby?"

"It seems like forever since we've heard her little voice, and I just want her to wake up and say something. I'm a doctor and I deal with life and death every day, but when it's someone you feel a responsibility to or care deeply about, it doesn't matter what your profession is. It is still extremely difficult."

"Yes it is tough, but we have to stay encouraged just for the moment when she will wake up and announce her presence." He turned Nadya to face him, kissed her gently on the lips, and hugged her to his chest.

With the arrival of the nurse for the evening,

they knew it was time for them to leave. Nadya and Sabien made their way back to the waiting area and when they arrived, it was like a party in there. Two long tables were pushed together and there was a buffet style setup of food from Serendipity sprawled across them. Several of Sabien's employees brought tons of food over from the restaurant, along with plates, cutlery, cups, and drinks.

"We figured since you wouldn't go to the food--we would bring the food to you," Dominic said to Sabien and Nadya. With their plates already made, they both sat down in their familiar corner to partake in the feast. The food was so good, and they were so hungry, but more than that, they were exhausted. And at one point, Nadine turned around to check on them and they had both fallen asleep, slumped over in their chairs with their heads laying on top of each other, plates leaning in their laps.

Nadine woke them both with a gentle tap on the shoulder, "Sweethearts, there is nothing you guys can do right now, why don't you go to Nadya's and rest since she's about a block away. Cori, Dominic, and I are going to be right here. Chloe and Justin are on their way and they will be spending the night. You have been in this hospital every waking moment. Go home get some nice hot showers, fresh clothes, and sleep in a comfortable bed. I promise we will call you immediately."

Nadya looked over at Sabien. It took a moment and he finally relented.

CHAPTER 34

After they mustered up enough energy to drive, Nadya and Sabien made their way to his house to get some clothes and then to hers to rest, since she was only minutes away from the hospital. They were barely able to make it to showering before plopping down on the bed, but they did.

When Nadya walked out of the bathroom, she found Sabien sprawled out over the bed in his boxers and t-shirt. She worked with his dead weight as much as possible to get him over to one side of the bed.

She then settled into bed next to him and was soon asleep as well, no longer able to fight the exhaustion that had consumed her.

Nadya woke from her sleep in the quiet, stillness of her room. She focused in on where she was and laid awake listening to Sabien's faint breathing next to her. It felt like an eternity since they arrived from the hospital, but it had only been a few hours.

She turned her body to face his, and traced the outline of his face with her fingertips. This was the most relaxed she'd seen him since the day of the wedding.

"I can feel your eyes on me," he whispered with his eyes still shut.

Nadya moved in slowly kissing his forehead, then his nose, then either cheek, before bringing her eyes back level with his.

His eyes fluttered open to find her staring at him, "How long have you been awake?" He looked around, noting the dim light of the moonlit sky coming in through the blinds.

"Furthermore, how long have I been out?"

Nadya grinned at him. "You needed it," she nuzzled her nose into his neck as he rubbed his index finger up and down her arm.

"I haven't been completely forthcoming about my past and what happened with me and Curtis," she paused and he doesn't move, so she continued. "I had an abortion," she said. Sabien stiffened and his serious gaze met hers. "Recently?" he asked, insinuating that she had aborted his child.

"No, no, no," Nadya answered now understanding his question. "Ten years ago. It was with Curtis. We made the decision together and he promised to be with me through the whole ordeal. Instead, he dropped me off afterward and that was the last day I talked to him. The reason I told you about this is because I still feel the pain of that loss."

Sabien remained silent.

"I can't completely relate to Vanessa and why she did what she did, but I think it has a lot to do with losing your son. She thinks you blame her and she probably blames herself. This type of pain can cause you to lose yourself. Even though I terminate my pregnancy, I felt like I had committed a horrible crime--I just wanted to crawl in a hole and die."

"You weren't entirely okay with the abortion," Sabien said.

"No, I wasn't. I did it because I felt there was no other option for me at the time. I still feel a huge sense of regret and grief."

"Do you think Vanessa feels this way?"

Nadya thought of her lying in the hospital bed undergoing a psychological evaluation. She had been in the mental ward for a week and Sabien was still refusing to see her. but she had gone to check on her. "I really believe that losing Jeremiah took a toll on Vanessa. It's especially hard when parent lose children to SIDS because they want answers and we can't give them any. We can't provide a reason for the loss."

Nadya reached over and took him by the hand. "I know it will take you some time to deal with this in your own way, but I wanted to share a part of me, which I hope will help you." Her voice trailed off and they laid in the dark watching each other.

"I love you," he confessed, as if he had said it a million times before.

"I love you too."

Nadya's phone startled them both. She clumsily grabbed it from her nightstand, "Hello."

"Serenity's awake," Chloe screamed.

"She's awake," she repeated. "Thank you, God."

Sabien leapt from the bed.

They dressed as fast as they could before flying out the door.

Sabien full of adrenalin, made it to the hospital like the only had to go from one side of the street to the other, and they floated through the hospital to the PICU.

When they arrived everyone was sitting in the lobby, but Nadya and Sabien barely said hello, as they bypassed them and headed straight to Serenity's room.

When they arrived, they find a nurse checking the measurements on the beeping machines, and depositing the tubing from the tubing, no longer needed. And propped up in the bed on a mound of pillows, sipping water through a straw, was his precious girl.

Sabien staggered for a minute, drinking her in. He hadn't known when or if he would ever see the twinkle of those bright brown eyes again. His eyes brimmed with tears as he went.

"Daddy," Serenity uttered, her voice hoarse. She coughed softly.

"Hello my Reese Cup. Daddy is so happy to see you," he said as he kissed her forehead.

"Can we go on our date now?" she asked, prompting laughter from him.

"Of course we can, baby. Anything you want."

"And can Dr. Nadya come?"

EPILOGUE

As the door to Granville Institution closed behind them, Nadya felt Sabien grab her hand and pull her closer to him.

They walked into the room and took their seats, as they had done in times past. This was not their first time within these particular four walls, but Sabien vowed the day Vanessa was committed, that he would put aside his anger and support her treatment. She had been for the past two years and this was the first time she'd asked that they come because she needed to speak with them--it was also the first time that she sounded almost like her old self.

Vanessa smiled at them when they entered the room.

Nadya noted a reflection of remorse in her

eyes, before they shifted to her left hand, taking note of her ring finger, adorned with a solitaire two carat pear-shaped, yellow diamond, and matching band.

Vanessa turned her head as she was led over to a metal folding chair at the visitor's table. An orderly stood near the exit door and another at a side entrance leading to the ward.

Vanessa cleared her throat and started in, "Thank you both for coming."

"Why are we here?" Sabien asked.

"Because I really need to tell you why." She took a deep breath, then continued, "I was in a really bad place after Jeremiah died. I was depressed and I thought I was going to lose my husband, too. I wanted to reach out to you, but you were covered in your own pain. You worked all of the time and I was alone. I'm not blaming you--just telling you why." Vanessa wiped away a tear. "This isn't easy for me."

"Take your time," he encouraged.

"When we found out we were pregnant again, I was a little apprehensive but you were so happy. We were finally back on track, but I was terrified."

As if on cue, Nadya felt a flutter in her own stomach and wasn't sure if it was butterflies or her own little one making her presence known.

"I just wanted so badly to be a good mother. I

didn't want to... to be the reason we lost another child.."

"It wasn't your fault. Vanessa, I never meant to make you feel like I blamed you for Jeremiah."

"I saw it every time you looked at me."

"It was your illness," Sabien said.

"Whether I was sick or not, I now recognize that the validation and love I sought hurt my daughter in the process… and for that I am deeply sorry. Sabien, I want you to know that I would never have done anything so evil if I had been in my right mind."

"I know that."

"I am very sorry and I have to ask one more thing of you. I need your forgiveness."

Nadya handed her a tissue.

"Vanessa, I forgive you. I just want you to get well."

She nodded. "I hope that one day Serenity will forgive me."

"She doesn't know what happened. I know that our daughter loves you and I won't ever do anything to change that."

She smiled at him. "Thank you."

Before they left, Vanessa reached out to grab Nadya's hand. "Thank you for taking care of my daughter. I can see that you love her as much as we do."

"Take care of yourself," she responded.

Nadya felt Sabien's body relax as if he had been holding his breath the whole time. When they were back in the car, he sat for a moment with his eyes closed, praying as a single tear rolled down his cheek.

She allowed him this moment. Although he and Vanessa were divorced, there was a part of him that would always care for her. This didn't both Nadya because she was secure in his love.

Nadya and Sabien got out of the car in front of Aunt Cori's house, and made their way inside. Before they could clear the doorway and dispose of their coats, Serenity rushed them, her iPad in hand.

"They're here. They're *here*." She hugged them both and plopped down on the sofa with her shoulders hunched over, as she swiped up the tablet screen with her finger.

"Hi Reese Cup. I take it you were waiting for us," her father said as he hung up his coat in the closet behind the front door and then took Nadya's to do the same.

"Aunt Cori and GiGi said we couldn't start without you. And I'm starving."

"Yes, I sure did. Serenity Reese, don't slouch, and sit lady like with that dress on," Nadine ordered as she walked in from the kitchen, heading toward the dining room with a platter of yeast rolls.

Serenity immediately straightened her posture and sat as poised as a debutante.

"Hurry up you two. The food won't stay hot for long, and Aunt Cori sure has put a nice spread together to celebrate our new addition."

Nadya and Sabien laughed in unison.

"Do as you're told, young lady," Sabien said to Serenity as he plopped down next to his daughter and hunched his shoulders over, teasing his daughter. He gave her a wink and she smiled back at him, and hopped up to join the rest of the family in the kitchen.

Nadya took a seat on Sabien's lap and leaned down to kiss him.

He released her lips and placed his hand gently on her stomach, "Now, Mrs. Mathews I know you said you think it's a girl, but I'm truly praying it's a boy, cause with GiGi, that little girl won't have a chance."

Nadya slapped him playfully on the back but she couldn't help but laugh because she knew he was right.

Sabien's spirited demeanor changed to a more serious one as he looked up into her eyes, "Have I told you lately how much I love you?"

"As a matter of fact, you did in the car. But feel free to tell me anytime."

I love you. I love you. I love you. *I love you,*" he whispered as he placed feathery kisses on her lips and down to her stomach, that was not yet showing signs that there was a life growing inside.

He kissed her stomach and was met by a low growling sound. "Looks like we've got a feisty one on our hands."

"More like hunger," Nadya quipped and rose up from his lap so they could head in for dinner.

Sabien stood up and hugged her from behind. "Thank you."

"For what?" she questioned.

"For sticking by me," he answered.

"Trust me. You couldn't get rid of me if you tried." She kissed her husband softly on the lips and they walked hand in hand towards the dining room to celebrate the news of their little bundle of joy.

If you or someone you know is struggling with
mental illness, you are not alone.

For more information please go to:

www.NAMI.org

Or

Contact the NAMI Helpline at:

800-950-NAMI (M-F, 10 AM - 6 PM ET)

CPSIA information can be obtained
at www.ICGtesting.com
Printed in the USA
LVOW08s2202220517
535483LV00001B/43/P